THE MIDNIGHT VISITORS

Also by Mike Attebery

The Grimwood Trilogy:
Flares
Ordinary World
The Midnight Visitors

Four Corners Thrillers:
Chokecherry Canyon
Firepower

Brick Ransom Thrillers:
Seattle On Ice
Bloody Pulp
Billionaires, Bullets, Exploding Monkeys

Standalone Novels:
On/Off
Rosé in Saint Tropez

The Midnight Visitors

Mike Attebery

Cryptic Bindings
Seattle

For
Steph and Charley

"Sometimes I'm here. Sometimes I'm not."

Part 1:
Year three

Timeline

1855 – Town of Grimwood is settled.

1869 – Ashton Grimwood founds Grimwood University.

1921 – Alan Grimwood is born.

1945 – Grimwood graduates and begins teaching at the University.

1955 – *Revenant* is published.

1969 – Founding of The Grimwood Writing Center.

1972 – Shooting on Grimwood campus.

1974 – *Black Robes* is published.

1978 – Alan Grimwood dies.

1981 – Grimwood's books go back into print.

1983 – Excerpts of *Doppelganger* are published.

1984 – *The Collected Stories of Alan Grimwood (1950-1978)* published.

...Present Day

1.

THE TRAIN RUMBLED PAST the dilapidated buildings on the out-skirts of town, its engine wheezing and shaking like a spent runner as it heaved to a stop in Grimwood station. Loren climbed to her feet to retrieve her bags, once more wondering why she ever thought these cross country train rides were a good idea.

While the rattle of the rails was meditative, the sheer scope of the nation's heartland could be overwhelming. As the train wound through the mountains and set off into the plains, a person's mind began to wander. The longer you rode the train, the more you felt *anything* was a viable possibility. You could get off in farmland just as easily as you could ride on to New York. Each stop on the route seemed like an invitation to explore some unexpected variation of your own life.

The time to think was welcome after a summer at home. Her parents were still in limbo – balanced between a frozen marriage and divorce – but she could see the way the pieces were shifting, and sooner or later her family's state of equilibrium would fall in on itself. Then everything would be different.

She was glad the odds of her being home for the crash were minimal. For that reason, if for nothing else, the train ride was a welcome reminder of the outside world, and broader horizons. But if she liked to imagine herself stepping off the train in an unfamiliar town, starting life anew, unencumbered and anonymous, Loren never doubted that Grimwood was her final destination; she had unfinished business there, and her heart would betray her if she ever tried to settle someplace else.

Over the past few months, as Loren worked in Puzzlebox Brewery's back office – getting the family business ready for the acquisition – and as she jogged along the farm roads outside Durango, she'd repeatedly heard one voice in her head, centering her thoughts, steadying her breathing, and pressing a thumb on the scale for every decision.

She needed to see Braden.

~

Hank stood by his car in front of the station as Loren walked out the double doors and into Grimwood's humid summer heat. He was watching a pair of freshman girls as they hailed a cab, and turned to see Loren walking his way just a split second *after* she'd seen where he was looking.

"You made it!" Hank exclaimed as he pulled off his sunglasses and hurried over to help with her bags. "How was your trip?"

"*Long,*" Loren said as she gave him a hug.

He walked around to the trunk of the car and started loading up her luggage. Loren *again* caught him sneaking a peak at the girls as they talked to their driver. She was mildly bemused, but decided not to call him out on his wandering eyes. "No Hannah?"

"She couldn't make it," Hank explained, his gaze no longer drifting as he climbed into the driver's seat and started the car. "Her co-op has been a little... overwhelming"

"How is she enjoying it?" Loren asked as she pulled the passenger door closed.

"What?"

"The co-op."

Hank sighed and pulled out into traffic. "We really shouldn't get into it."

"Oh," Loren said, taken aback. "It's not going well?"

"To put it mildly. Don't worry, she'll tell you *all* about it. It's one of her favorite topics these days. That and the new neighbors."

"She doesn't like them either?"

Hank gave her a look. "They're noisy, but they're not *that* bad. We could do a lot worse with how many students are looking for off campus housing right now."

"I can imagine…" Loren said knowingly.

In mid-August, just after the conclusion of Summer quarter, a malfunction in the emergency sprinkler system in Judy Valentine Hall – Grimwood University's largest residence tower – had flooded the building and wreaked havoc on the housing plans for the upcoming school year. The timing and location of the mishap couldn't have been planned for greater destruction. It had occurred when virtually no one was on campus, and what's more, none of the usual notifications or alarms were tripped to notify the fire department or campus safety that anything was amiss. The result: When every fire suppression sprinkler on the top floor of the building inexplicably turned on, no one knew about it for the better part of a weekend, which gave the steady stream of water time to build, until it began cascading down through the walls and ductwork, making its way down each and every floor of the building in a slow but steady trickle, bringing down drop-ceilings, saturating drywall, destroying carpet and furnishings, and ultimately, knocking out almost a quarter of the on campus housing just two weeks before everyone was set to return to campus for Autumn quarter.

In order to ensure the incoming freshman would have on campus housing, notice was sent out to two thirds of the returning students informing them that their housing arrangements for the upcoming school year could not be guaranteed. That had included Loren, Elissa, Brooke, and – Loren assumed – Braden, but she hadn't spoken to him in almost two months.

Elissa and Brooke had found a two bedroom place for the summer, which they were able to extend indefinitely, with Loren taking over the spare bedroom once she ensured it was *not* a unit in the Racquet Club apartments – the hellhole she and Brooke had shared the previous summer.

"Do you need to stop anywhere, or should I just take you to your new digs?"

"New digs would be great if you can."

"That is not a problem," Hank said. "It's literally across the street from our place."

"Really?" Loren asked. "So, what is our apartment like?"

"It's not bad. Certainly better than your place last summer."

"That's all I need to know." Loren breathed a sigh of relief as they turned onto The Avenue and headed into town.

She watched the familiar sights sliding into view. Coffee shops. Restaurants. The bookstore. Though she hadn't seen these places in months, it felt like she'd just left. Brick's was on the corner as Hank turned the car onto 75th and pulled to a stop in front of The Dean Apartments on Greenwood Avenue. They climbed out of the car, and Hank walked around to open the trunk.

"Hopefully you recognize our place," he said – pointing to the building behind him, then sweeping his hand around to the apartments across the street. "And that's you guys."

"That *is* close."

"I need to get ready for my shift at the restaurant," Hank explained. "Are you OK getting to your place?"

"Of course." Loren picked up her bags. "I got across the country by myself, I should be all right crossing the street."

"Hannah is trying to get everyone together at Brick's tonight if you're interested. It won't be until late, like nine o'clock, but I know Brooke and Elissa are coming. I haven't heard anything from Braden though."

"That sounds great," Loren said. "I'll see you at nine."

"Oh, hey, I almost forgot to give you these." Hank pulled a set of keys from his pocket and tossed them to her. "I'll catch you later."

"Thanks, Hank."

~

Loren let herself into the building, walked upstairs, and opened the door to Apartment D. The living room was sparsely outfitted with a TV, a beaten up couch, and a well-worn coffee table. The kitchen was at the far end of the space. A beaded curtain hung across the entrance to a short hallway on the left. The first door in the corridor was closed, but the second was open, letting in a stream of warm light. Loren walked to the end and looked inside, immediately recognizing the boxes she'd left behind for the summer. Brooke and Elissa had set her up with a box spring and mattress and a few random pieces of furniture. Sitting atop the mattress, with a note taped to the glass, was a familiar object: Brooke's lava lamp from freshman year. Loren picked it up and read the note:

"Loren – Welcome back! I thought this might help you feel at home. (Elissa is not a fan.) ~Brooke"

Loren smiled, set the lamp on the window ledge, and plugged it in. Then she turned to the boxes and started unpacking. Aside from the bed, there was a beaten up desk and chair, and a small, collapsible bookshelf. None of it was pretty, but it would get the job done. She'd eventually need to find a few more things to make the place comfortable, but this was already several steps up from Racquet Club.

There was no dresser, but the closet had a few shelves and some discarded hangers, so she unpacked her clothes and put them away, along with her books and a collection of notepads. Loren flipped through her handwritten pages as she organized her desk, reviewing some of the pieces she'd produced over the summer. She had proposed a series of interconnected short stories for her Junior Thesis, and gained approval despite the misgivings expressed by a few members of The Writing Center's faculty. Loren got the feeling it was put up or shut up time if she was serious about her prospects in the program. She was excited to type up her stories and flesh them out over the course of the quarter. It would be interesting to see what she had on her hands by the end of Fall quarter. Either way, it felt good to be creating again.

Going over Braden's novel had awakened her to the inherent possibilities of revision. His book was good, but she felt her changes would make it significantly better. Whether or not he incorporated her edits remained to be seen, but revising someone else's work had given her an eye-opening understanding of what she could do to strengthen her own writing; it had also made Braden's subsequent silence especially disappointing. Aside from a short note after she mailed the revised pages back to him, she had heard nothing from him over the course of the summer.

Still, she was excited to see him.

~

Loren headed to the bookstore after lunch to pick up her work schedule. The street was quiet, virtually abandoned in the heat of midday. The atmosphere reminded her of the previous summer, when, for reasons she didn't entirely understand, she'd frequently felt a palpable sense of loneliness during the days.

Despite her friendships at the bookstore, and her one-time relationship with the owner's son, when she thought of R. K. Phillips Booksellers, more than anyone else, Loren thought of Braden. After all, he'd alerted her to the job in the first place, and even when he wasn't working, he was always there in spirit. Being there without him just felt odd.

Air-conditioning washed over her as the bell on the front door jingled. The main floor was relatively quiet. The sounds of the lunchtime crowd murmured from the café in the back as Loren headed up the stairs to the back office.

She slipped past Mary Ellen's desk, only to do a double take at the sight of a bearded man in his mid-30s, with dark, receding hair and a beard, who was seated at the manager's desk, eating a tuna sandwich.

"Can I help you," he asked in a thick Irish brogue.

"Hi, umm, I was just looking to get my schedule from Mary Ellen…"

His eyes narrowed. "And you are?"

"Loren. I work here during the school year. I'm just back from summer break."

"Ah, Loren… Austin. Right?" He set his sandwich down and reached for a stack of papers above the desk. "I just finished working you into the schedule for evenings."

"I'm sorry." Now it was Loren's turn to be confused. "I don't think we've met…"

"Oh, right." He stood and handed her a copy of the schedule. "Karl Ryan. I'm the new manager."

"Hi." Loren said as she shook Karl's hand. "I didn't realize Mary Ellen was planning on leaving."

"Yeah, I'm not sure she really had much of a plan, but she left… From what I can gather, some things went down…"

"I see."

Knowing Mary Ellen's temper, Loren could only imagine what might have happened, but her best guess was that the former manager had butted heads with Roxanne one time too many.

"Let me know if you need me to make any changes," Karl said as Loren glanced at the schedule.

"It looks pretty good," she said.

"You don't happen to know who Braden McNutt is, do you?"

Loren smiled. "I do."

"I think he's supposed to be back this week too," Karl said as he handed her another print-out and sat back down. "If you happen to see him before I do, could you give him his schedule as well?"

"Sure."

"Nice to meet you, Loren," Karl said before returning to his sandwich.

"You too," Loren replied as she continued through the offices.

She glanced over Braden's schedule as she headed down the back stairs, looking to see if they had any days in common. Now that she was back, she felt a sudden and unexpected swell of irritation thinking about the way Braden had gone silent on her.

Who was he to just ignore her for the entire summer?

She pushed the door open at the bottom of the back stairs, self-righteous indignation building by the second as she stepped out into the parking lot.

And then, there he was, sitting on the hood of an old, dark green BMW, as if he was waiting for her.

"Braden-"

He looked up and smiled. "Hi."

"How did you get here?"

"I finally got my grandfather's car working again." He banged his palm on the hood. "What do you think?"

Loren nodded her approval. *"I like it."*

Whatever fleeting anger had welled up in her chest instantly evaporated.

She walked over and gave him a hug. "It's good to see you."

"You too."

"When did you get back?"

"Yesterday," he said.

"And were you going to tell anyone?"

"Of course. I was just getting settled into my apartment. You know how it is, I was expecting to have one more year in the dorms." He locked her in his gaze. "Why? When did *you* get back?"

"This morning."

His brow furrowed. "What time is it now, like one o'clock?"

"That sounds about right."

"You've been in Grimwood a few hours at the *most!* It's not like you've been back for days and I've been hiding from you the whole time.""

No. She thought to herself. *Just most of the summer.*

"Still, I would've liked to have known you were here," Loren said sincerely.

"Did someone pick you up at the station?" Braden asked warily.

He was wondering if Cole was back in the picture.

"Hank gave me ride."

Braden's face brightened. "Oh yeah?"

"He drove me from the station to the apartment I'm sharing with Brooke and Elissa."

"Where's that?"

"Perkins Green. It's really close. Where's your place?

Braden smiled and looked over his shoulder, pointing across the way to a red brick building.

"It's right over there."

"Wow. That's *really* close."

Their eyes met.

"Would you like to see it?" Braden asked.

"Sure…"

She said it like a question, wondering where this might lead.

~

The lock on the back door didn't look the most secure, but the building itself seemed fairly well maintained. No fortress, but certainly not a slum. They made their way up the back stairs, emerging in the drab, first floor hallway, which was covered with green, industrial-style carpet and lit by dim wall sconces. Braden stopped at the last door on the right and pulled out a set of keys. He looked back at Loren, his expression almost sheepish.

"It's just a studio," he said. "But I think it's pretty decent for a last minute find."

Loren smiled nervously. "It's nicer than Racquet Club, Braden. I can tell you that already."

Braden opened the door and held it for Loren as she stepped inside. A curious energy crackled in the air between them as she passed by.

Other than shifts at the bookstore, Loren couldn't think of the last time they'd been alone together, just the two of them. Her stomach was suddenly tense with excitement.

The entrance to the bathroom was just to the right of the front door. An open kitchen was a few steps past that. The rest of the unit was one sparsely-furnished living space. Aside from an unmade bed and two bar stools at the counter, there was little in the way of furniture. She noted the stacks of books on the floor beside the bed, and the writing station set up on the counter. Notebooks. Pens and paper. The manuscript with her edits marked in red. All of these were neatly stacked beside a small, black laptop.

"I like it," she said.

"Thanks."

"You got a new computer."

"I did." He followed her gaze to the manuscript. "Thank you again for looking over the first draft."

"It was fun." She crossed the room to the windows, and looked down at the back lot. "I hope there was something useful in my notes."

"They've been a big help," he said. "I really liked your edits."

Loren reached for the wand on the window blinds, rotating the blades to a sixty degree angle as Braden watched her uncertainly.

She walked back to him, nodding toward the counter. "I like your writing setup, too."

"Thanks," he replied as he opened one of the cabinets and took down a bag of Caffe Vita. "Do you want some coffee?"

"Sure…" Loren said, the word once more sounding like a question.

Braden spoke quickly as he prepped the machine. "I figure I'll still do most of my work at the library, but it will be nice to have the option of staying close to home sometimes. Especially if the winter is anything like it was last year."

The smell of ground coffee hung in the air as Braden started the brewer. He turned around to find Loren standing behind him, her expression at ease. His eyes settled on the subtle laugh lines at the corners of her mouth.

She set her fingers on his waist, pushing his hands aside as she stepped closer. "Is this ok?" she asked.

"Sure…" he said, echoing her tone from a moment earlier.

Loren kissed him gently, bringing her hands to the sides of his face, feeling the stubble along his jawline.

He kissed her back. Nervously.

She slipped her hand in his, leading him over to the bed, where they lay on the bare mattress – still hot from the midday sun.

Braden ran his fingers through her hair and looked into her eyes. "Do you have any idea how long I've wanted to do that?"

"Too long," she said, and kissed him again.

The sun slipped past the windows as they lay together on Braden's bed, making out until the light through the blinds glowed pink.

"Can I interest you in a cup of burned coffee?" Braden asked when he finally got up from the bed and headed for the kitchen.

"I think I might pass." Loren laughed as she self-consciously straightened her shirt.

"Suit yourself," Braden replied. He poured himself a mug and sat on the corner of the bed.

Loren looked at the clock. "Hey, I told Hank I'd meet everyone for dinner at nine. Do you want to go?"

"Of course."

"We'd better get going."

Braden brushed his fingers through his mussed hair. "How do I look?"

Loren kissed him and gave him the once over. "Like you've got a secret."

~

"How are you roomie?" Brooke asked as she slipped out of the booth at Brick's to give Loren a hug.

"I'm good. I got a chance to swing by the apartment."

"-And?"

"Pretty nice digs."

"That's what we thought."

"I guess that makes us roomies now, too," Elissa added.

"I think you're right." Loren replied. She glanced toward Hank and Hannah, who were seated at the end of the booth discussing something. "Hey, guys. How was your summer?"

Hannah rolled her eyes. "I was just filling everyone in-"

"*Hot,*" Hank interjected, cutting Hannah off.

Loren looked from one to the other, trying to gauge the mood between them.

"Hot?"

"I work in a restaurant with no AC," Hank said. "You get the idea."

"We *just* ordered some food," Elissa noted. "Let me see if I can flag Betty down."

"That would be great," Braden replied. "I'm starved."

"I'm pretty hungry too," Loren said as she made eye contact with Hannah. "Let me get an order in, then I want to hear all about your co-op." She slid into the booth and moved down to the end.

"Well, I'm definitely getting the Brick Plate," Braden said as he slid into the booth beside her.

"*Really?*" Loren exclaimed.

"Why are you surprised?" Brooke asked. "Braden *always* gets the Brick Plate,"

"Yeah, I know. I just thought he might want something a little less… *assertive* tonight. "

She was really more concerned how the restaurant's signature meal might affect the rest of their evening.

Brooke glanced around the table, noting the ease with which Braden and Loren had so quickly settled in beside each other. It also hadn't escaped her attention that the two of them arrived together. Either they'd finally established a comfortable balance, or something was afoot.

Once the latecomers ordered their food, Hannah launched into a lengthy recap of her co-op experience over the Summer quarter, managing to hold the table captive until their food arrived. "So yeah, it's a structural engineering firm," she concluded as Betty set their plates down. "But it *feels* like a labor camp. I cannot wait until I'm done."

As if waiting for the first break in the conversation – which he was – Hank immediately jumped in. "Elissa, how has your summer at Atlas Structural been?"

"Eh. It's not the most exciting work in the world, but the pay is nice. I can't really complain."

"How refreshing," Hank said.

Brooke's eyes darted to Hannah, then across to Loren, who

visibly winced at the tension coming from Hank and Hannah's corner of the table.

"So, Loren, Braden," Brooke asked mischievously. "What have *you guys* been up to since you got back to town?"

"Oh, you know…" Loren replied, trying to gauge Brooke's intonation as she set her hand on Braden's leg under the table. "Just catching up."

~

The light was fading as the six friends gathered on the street in front of the restaurant after dinner.

"Well, it's good to see everyone" Hank said.

"Loren, do you want to walk back with us?" Elissa asked.

Loren's thoughts were racing as she tried to come up with an excuse to slip away with Braden.

"Loren, I was thinking of heading up to the store to pick up my work schedule if you wanted to walk with me," Braden offered.

"Yeah!" Loren said, perhaps a bit too enthusiastically. "I've been meaning to pick mine up as well."

Brooke's eyes narrowed suspiciously as she and the rest of the group turned to go.

Braden looked at Loren once the others were gone. After avoiding suspicious eye contact throughout dinner, it was a relief to drop the charade.

"By the way, I have your work schedule," Loren said as she took his hand. Their fingers slid together naturally.

"What do you want to do now?" Braden asked.

"Head back to your place."

"That's sounds good to me."

~

It was close to midnight by the time Loren walked in the door at her new apartment. Brooke and Elissa were stretched out on the couch in the living room, watching TV.

"Hi, Loren," Elissa said without looking away from the TV.

"Hey," Loren answered as she sat on the floor to watch with them.

Brooke's eyes went to the clock.

The show came to a close, the end credits crawling up the screen as Elissa got to her feet. "Oh, Felicity. Will you ever learn?" She leaned down and gave Brooke a kiss.

"You going to bed?" Brooke asked.

"Yep, back to the salt mines bright and early tomorrow." Elissa answered. "Don't stay up too late. You want to be awake for the first day of classes."

"And practice," Brooke noted.

"That's right. I'll miss that!"

"Really?" Brooke asked. "You'll miss the crack of dawn run?"

"Well, I'll miss seeing everybody, let's put it that way. Have a good night, Loren."

"You too." Loren said as Elissa closed the bedroom door.

Loren's gaze drifted from the door to Brooke, who was watching her expectantly, like a coyote eyeing the entrance to a prairie dog mound.

"*What?*" Loren asked.

"*Something happened…*"

"With?"

"You and Braden."

Loren fought back a smile.

"Spill it."

"…We're just seeing where it goes."

"And how was it? Did you…?"

"Boy, you don't beat around the bush. We haven't gotten to that yet. The lead up has been pretty great though."

~

Hank turned to Braden as they waited for their drinks at the bookstore cafe. "Do you ever worry he's been forgotten?"

"Who?" Braden asked as the barista slid two coffees across the counter.

"Jason. And are you *trying* to prove my point."

"Of course not. I don't think he's been forgotten at all," Braden said.

They walked out the back of the store, sipping their drinks as they walked around to The Avenue.

"We're living our lives, but I know we all think about him. It's hard not to. He's the reason most of us became friends in the first place."

"I think of him in every production class," Hank said. He stopped suddenly at the corner.

"Did you forget something?"

"You know, I thought I saw him once… after it happened. Does that sound crazy?"

Braden shook his head. "Not at all."

Hank gave him a funny look.

The signal changed and they started across the street toward campus.

"Whenever we discussed starting up our own label, I always figured I'd be the one to run the business side of things, and Jason would scout the bands and work with the talent. He was so good with people."

"You know, Hank, you're pretty good with people yourself. You've got the same skills, you're just operating at a different…pitch."

"Why does that sound like a back-handed compliment?"

"It's not meant to be," Braden laughed. "But I know what you mean. My point is that you might have to wear both hats, but you could still make it happen. No question. What would you call your label anyway?"

Hank sighed. "I think I'd *have* to go with Jason's first choice. Cradle to the Groove Records."

"You mean 'grave.'"

"That's what I said, but he had his heart set on *Groove*."

"Cradle to the Groove…" Braden murmured. "I guess that's as good a name as any. Plus, like you said, you don't really have a choice about it. You've gotta use that one."

~

"So wait, *did* he actually see Jason?" Loren asked as they headed into The Writing Center.

"He said he *thought* he saw him once," Braden emphasized. "I didn't press him for details, but I thought it was interesting."

"Totally. First Hannah, then Hank."

"The skeptics are cracking. How do you think those two are doing by the way?"

Loren sighed. "Not great."

"There was some palpable tension at the table last night."

"Living with someone who detests what they're doing is not a recipe for a good time."

They filed into the auditorium with the rest of the Junior class, taking their seats near the back of the lecture hall.

"Have *you* ever seen Jason?" Braden asked out of the blue.

Loren shook her head.

"Ever feel him around?"

"Nope."

"Me neither. Maybe that's a good thing, right? No loose ends."

"At least, none that involve us," Loren said wistfully.

A rustle of activity drifted through the room as the first class of the year began.

"It's been a long time since we had a lecture together," Braden observed.

When Professor Price walked into the room, it felt to Loren as if they'd come full circle.

Braden, nudged her knee as he leaned over and whispered, "Still wearing green."

Their freshman year, Braden noticed Professor Price's habit of always wearing a touch of emerald green. Today it was the sweater under his blazer.

Price set his books down and surveyed the room. Once everyone was at attention, he began.

"I believe this is the first time I've had many of you since The Novel in your freshman year. I trust that a lot has happened to you over the course of the last two years – in your classes and in your lives – if you're fortunate, much of it has been positive, but if not, well, my more mercenary writer instincts say *'You can work with that!'*"

A wave of laughter rippled through the room.

"The purpose of this program will be to assist each of you in the development, creation, and revision of your junior thesis. We're moving away from reading and studying writing, and leaping into the work that each of you has decided will see you through your careers. Grimwood makes you settle on your major early, but I cannot say this clearly enough, if at this point you're feeling anxious about your skills as a writer, if you're questioning your stamina, discipline, focus, and even your very voice…" He looked around for emphasis… "Then congratulations, you're definitely a member of the tribe. Self-doubt, the inner turmoil, it *never* goes away."

Loren felt the knot in her stomach loosen slightly. Unlike Braden, the bulk of her writing over the last two years had been entirely related to course assignments. The stories she worked on over the summer were the first personal, creative work she'd embarked on in ages. It had felt good to create again, but she still heard that little voice of doubt whispering in her ear at times. Price's words were reassuring, even if they reinforced her fear that the second-guessing never went away.

"You know, we've never discussed either of our thesis projects," Braden said.

A girl in the next row turned and scowled at them.

"We'll talked about it later," Loren whispered back. "Are you working tonight?"

Braden nodded. "You?"

She shook heard head. "Why don't you come over to my place afterward. We'll get up to speed."

"Sounds good."

"Over the next two quarters, you will be working on your projects, meeting with me for one on one check-ins, and pre-senting you work to your classmates during lectures. In the third quarter, class sessions will end, and each of you will work with members of the faculty to finalize your thesis before turning in the final work. If we're doing everything properly, this should be an exciting and yes, tiring time for all of us. Faculty *included.* In addition to the work on your projects, we'll *also* be reading and examining one work over the course of the first quarter."

A low groan rumbled in the room.

"I know. I know," Price said sarcastically. "God forbid writers should read as well as write."

~

There were still a few Krispy Kremes left in the breakroom. They'd arrived warm that morning, their bearer happily discussing a TV singing competition the night before. The box had sat on the counter in the hours since, as office workers quietly went about the day, absentmindedly grazing on pastries.

She'd eaten two donuts while they were still warm. After her boss stopped by her cubicle to drop off the day's "to-do list," Hannah had instinctively hopped to her feet and headed back to the kitchenette, where she again lifted the lid and pondered the expanding grease ring on the bottom of the cardboard box. With a mix of base excitement and quiet self-loathing, she grabbed a cold third donut and shoved it in her mouth, licking flakes of hardened sugar glaze from the corners of her mouth as she returned to her desk.

She hated this job.

Two years ago, if someone had asked her if she was excited for college, she would have expressed nothing short of impatience at her wish to be done with school and set loose on the workplace. After one quarter at her architectural co-op, with another quarter just beginning, she couldn't imagine what she'd been thinking.

So far, this was *not* the work for her. There was nothing inspiring or satisfying about what she was doing, She felt like a lackey. The self-expression, the expected sense of urgency she'd always assumed awaited her in the working world, they were nowhere to be found. Life was nothing but a 9 to 5 grind, with bad coffee and emotion-smothering junk food.

The moment she returned to her seat, Hannah's thought returned to the last donut remaining in the box. How long it would be before someone snagged that final raised glazed. If she went back in a few minutes, maybe she could get it.

~

Braden closed up the store and was out on The Ave by 9:30. The air was humid and warm, still feeling very much like summer as he walked the few short blocks to Perkins Green Apartments. His heartbeat accelerated as he approached the building and rang the buzzer.

"Hello?" Loren's tinny voice asked from the call box.

"It's me."

She buzzed him in.

The door to apartment D was unlocked. Braden stepped inside, surveyed the darkened living room, and locked the door behind him. He stood in the hallway, trying his best to quietly remove his sneakers as he waited for his eyes to adjust to the darkness, then he made his way to the living room. It smelled like Loren and Brooke's previous dorm rooms. One of the bedroom doors was closed. Elissa and Brooke must have gone to bed already. A sliver of warm light glowed from the other door which stood open a crack. Braden crossed the room and knocked gently on the doorframe.

"Hi," Loren said as she opened the door and stepped into view.

She was dressed in a nightshirt with buttons running down the front, most of which were unfastened. Braden smiled and glanced around the room. Candles flickered on the window sill beside a slowly oscillating fan and a lava light he recognized from Loren's freshman dorm room.

Loren closed the door behind him and stepped closer, her shirt slipping open as she led him to the bed.

"Is this too soon?" Braden asked.

Loren shook her head and kissed him. "It should have happened a long time ago."

~

Brooke was up early the next morning. She padded to the kitchen, where she filled a mug with coffee from the pot Elissa had brewed before she left for work. Then she headed back to her room, drinking black coffee as she threw on her clothes and got ready for crew practice. She grabbed a granola bar and her keys and headed for the door, stopping suddenly as she noticed a pair of men's sneakers on the floor in the front hallway.

Brooke smiled as she slipped out the door.

She had a pretty good guess who those belonged to.

2.

"Come on. This is not that big a deal," Hank said as he walked from the kitchen to the closet to get ready. "Just grab a cup on the way."

"That's easy for you to say, Hank," Hannah said as she marched across the apartment after him. "But if you *knew* we were out of coffee, you should have picked some up yesterday."

"I'm sorry. I forgot. OK? I'll get some tonight."

"That really doesn't do me any good now, though, does it?"

Hank pulled on a T-shirt and did his best to ignore the last comment. These absurd domestic disputes had become a part of their regular morning routine, and he wasn't sure what he could do to stop them.

"Jesus," he muttered under his breath.

"What was that?"

"Look, I know you're unhappy with this co-op. But you don't have to take it out on me, all right? If you hate your major so much, you still have time to change it."

"What am I supposed to do, just drop everything and start over?!"

He raised his hands in resignation. "Yeah. Get a fresh start. I'd support you."

Hannah stared back at him, pokerfaced, then turned around and slammed the bedroom door. The noise reverberated in the apartment as Hank grabbed his backpack and left.

The argument weighed on his thoughts as he swung by the bookstore café, grabbing an espresso and feeling just a little bit guilty as he took his first sip and savored the tingle of caffeine. He bought a couple pounds of coffee to go along with his order, and asked the girl behind the counter to grind them for him before he left.

Campus was bustling, with everyone seeming slightly more energized by the first hints of fall in the air. Hank had two lectures that day – a production class and a liberal arts gut course. By the end of the first session, all thoughts of domestic bickering had slipped from his mind.

Afterwards, he grabbed a quick lunch at the SAU and headed to The Ave for a shift at Red Tomato. This was an unusually packed day. Most weekdays he had one or two morning classes, followed by a few hours tossing pizzas at Red Tomato, or a shift at the campus radio station, WGRM. Today he was scheduled to work at both.

Red Tomato was hopping, with returning students grabbing tables and pitchers of beer as they shared pizzas and studied. Hank finished his shift around eight, fixed himself a seven-inch pie, quietly pulled himself a beer, and ate dinner in the breakroom.

The light was fading as he cut across the grassy hillside to the campus radio station and walked into the building for the first time that year.

"There he is!" Howard called as Hank strolled down the hall. "Hank, this is Rachel," he said, pointing to an attractive blond-haired girl standing beside him. "Rachel is a freshman in the music production program. Tonight's her first night working at the station. I thought you could show her around, let her sit in on your broadcast and see how it's done."

Rachel stood to the side, quietly brushing her hair behind her ears and sneaking peeks at her shoes. She looked up and caught Hank's eye, her face flushing slightly as she flashed an intoxicating smile.

"Sure," Hank said. "It will be nice to have some company for the late shift."

"Great." Howard started back for his office. "If you need anything, I'll be around for another ten minutes, then I'm heading down to the Pig 'n Whistle."

Hank clapped his hands together once they were alone. "So, did he give you the tour yet?"

"Not really," she said.

"Well, let me show you around." He glanced at the hall clock. "Then we'd better get into the booth. I'm on the air in a few minutes."

For someone who prided himself on his unflappability, Hank was unusually aware of his mannerisms as he took Rachel around the building. It felt as though he was giving the tour in the third person, watching himself watching *her* out of the corner of his eye, cringing a little as he turned on the charm, and smiling happily when his efforts seemed to hit home. He experienced a brief sense of déjà vu as he pointed her to the coffee maker and shared the location of Howard's bottle of Kahlua. It reminded him of his first night working at the station with Jason.

By the time he sat down to begin his show, Hank was invigorated for his broadcast in a way he hadn't been in ages, and somewhat taken aback at how enchanted he was with this new girl.

At the end of the night, after spending the two-hour broadcast talking with Rachel between song introductions, Hank felt an unsettling level of guilt at just how much he was crushing on this girl. Her blues eyes, and the subtle folds under her lower lids were burned in his brain as he said goodnight and locked the door.

"Thanks for showing me the ropes," Rachel said as they stood on the front walk.

"It was fun. Maybe we can do it again some time."

"I hope so," Rachel said as she spun on her heel and headed into the darkness of campus.

Hank walked back down the hill to The Ave. Conflicted or not, it had been a pleasant evening. Hopefully their schedules at the station would cross again.

~

"Someone on the bus stank. It was unbearable, like a moldy washcloth, buried under a sink full of dishes…" Karl looked up from the book he was holding. "Pfft! No thank you!" he said, tossing it back on the shelving cart as Dan came around the corner with a handful of books.

Loren laughed and rummaged through the cart.

"What are you guys doing?" Dan asked.

"Reading first sentences and deciding if we'd be willing to give the whole book a chance," Karl said.

"What about this one," Loren began, as she flipped to the front of another book. "A coyote scampered across the street and disappeared into the bushes as the car's headlights swept across the dirt parking lot. The vehicle pulled up to the front of the crumbling stucco building, exhaust fumes visible in the wintery desert air."

"I like it," Dan exclaimed. "Sounds like a moody start to a good mystery."

Karl looked unimpressed. "I don't know, it could be great or it could be a poor man's *Chinatown*. I'd need to read more…"

Dan reached over and peeked at the cover, which showed a Southwest canyon dripping with crude oil. "Yeah, I'd read that."

"Sounds good to me, too," Loren said.

This was her first night back at the store, and her first shift working with the new manager, whose style appeared to be a 180 degree shift from the totalitarian management approach of the previous regime. Whereas Mary Ellen preferred a reign of retail rage, Karl was more interested in talking books and getting to know the staff while they worked together to keep the customers happy. So far, it made for a much more relaxed evening at the bookstore.

"All right. I've got it," Karl announced. He held up a book with an artsy, out of focus shot of a figure trudging through a snowstorm. "There was a sliver of metal in his brain… He could feel it *scraping* against the tissue, *biting* into the swollen gray pulp…" He hit the verbs like drumbeats and hung on the more grotesque details. "It hurt like hell. Every movement, every breath, sent a wave of pain rushing through his head…" He looked up dramatically, stabbing at the page with his index finger. "Now *that* I would read! In fact, I think I will."

"I dunno…" Dan replied. "I still like that coyote book."

"Suit yourself," Karl said as he headed for the stairs. "But I'm taking this one home with me tonight."

"How is it going Loren?" Dan asked when it was just the two of them.

"Good. I've missed this place."

"I always like it when all of you Grimwood folks are back for the year."

"Yeah, me too. It's funny how *this* starts to feel like home, and *home* starts to feel like being away… Speaking of which. I have sort of an awkward question for you."

"Is this about Braden?" Dan asked.

"Uh…no."

"Is it about Cole?"

"Yeah, actually, it is." She looked at him with a funny smile on her face. "Boy, you're back in that receiving room half the day, but you don't miss a trick, do you?"

"I'm like the Wizard of Oz."

"I guess so. Anyway, I was looking at the schedule, trying to sort of prepare myself for any uncomfortable interactions, but I didn't see his name anywhere."

"You don't know?"

"Know what?"

"Cole left at the start of the summer. He talked Roxanne into picking up the tab for a trip to Europe."

"Oh, wow. No, I didn't hear that. How long will he be gone?"

"It sounds like it's an indefinite change of scenery."

"Like, he's not coming back?"

"Look, I'll level with you" Dan said, motioning to the back room. "I just sit at my desk back there, and try my damnedest to eavesdrop on everyone's conversations." Loren laughed as he continued. "All I know is that from the way I've heard Roxanne talking, it sounds like she shoved him out of the nest, but he's still on the family charge accounts, so she's doesn't expect him back here anytime soon."

"Huh," Loren said.

She was relieved, but this was going to take some getting used to.

"I hope I'm not telling you anything you didn't want to hear…" Dan said as he headed for the back room.

"No, not at all. That's good to know."

~

"If you really want to know how to stir fry, come over here," Elissa said, moving aside to let Brooke step in front of the stove.

"Don't I need those… spatula thingies?" Brooke said, motioning to the implements in her girlfriend's hands. "What are those called, anyway?"

"This is the shovel, and this is the ladle." Elissa placed a handle in each of Brooke's hands and stepped behind her, gently placing her hands on her girlfriend's forearms as she moved in closer. "You just lift and flip the ingredients gracefully."

"Gracefully?" Brooke murmured as she turned to kiss Elissa's cheek. "I don't do graceful. I'm from New York."

"What are you talking about? New Yorkers are graceful. Audrey Hepburn was graceful."

"She was born in Belgium."

"But her character in *Breakfast at Tiffany's* was graceful."

Brooke hesitated, but she couldn't help herself. "According to Truman Capote, Holly Golightly was a prostitute."

Elissa kissed her neck. "Prostitutes can't be graceful?"

Brooke turned around "I'm not even sure the movie was filmed in New York."

Elissa laughed. "Are you just *trying* to be contrary?"

The front door opened and closed in the front hall. When they looked up, Loren was standing in the kitchen.

"Hey guys." She set her bag on the counter and walked over to the fridge. "Don't stop on account of me, I'll be out of here in a second."

"Don't be silly," Brooke said, giving Elissa another quick kiss and returning to the stove. "Are you hungry? We're making a big batch."

Loren peeked into the wok. "Are you sure you have enough?"

"We have a *ton*," Brooke said.

"Then yeah, that would be awesome."

Elissa took down three plates and set them beside the stove.

Loren looked on as her roommates made their way around the kitchen. There was certainly chemistry in *that* relationship. Sparks were practically shooting through the air between them as they finished preparing the meal. She hoped she and Braden might have that same connection two years from now. With any luck, he would come by again tonight.

3.

WEEKS LATER, LOREN AWOKE to the sound of hot coffee being poured into a mug. She stretched her legs out under the smooth cotton sheets of Braden's bed, then curled up tighter, huddling against the morning chill. When she finally opened her eyes and looked across the room, all she saw was Braden's back as he sat at the counter, hunched over a stack of papers, marking up changes in red ink.

He reached for his coffee and took a swig. Something about the gesture pulled invisible marionette strings in Loren's arms and legs, triggering another full body stretch and an involuntary yawn.

He looked back at her. "Good morning."

She smiled, groaning softly. Nothing about her was entirely awake yet. "That coffee smells delicious."

Braden poured a cup and brought it over to her.
"Thanks."

She took a sip as he returned to the counter, then she turned to look out the studio window. The trees were beginning to change colors. The green leaves glowing softly, the edges singed a pale orange.

"What do you think we're doing, Braden?"

"What do you mean?" The barstool creaked as he turned to face her. "What do *you* think we're doing?"

"We're just seeing how it goes, right?"

She could practically *hear* herself waffling.

"No we're not."

"We're not?" She asked, caught off guard by the surprise in her own voice.

"I'm all in, and I think you are too. As far as I'm concerned, this is it."

She held the warm mug in her hands as she watched Braden's expression. He didn't flinch. The tone of his words and the certainty in his voice were both frightening and immensely reassuring.

She set the mug on the floor, wrapped the sheets around her, and walked silently across the room to him. As their eyes met, she saw the briefest flash of worry in Braden's eyes, concern that he might have said too much.

That look pained her, and as she leaned forward to kiss him, she realized that he was right. She was all in too.

* * *

The heater in Hank's old car took a long time to get working. He'd switched it on as soon as he left to pick Hannah up at her co-op, but it was only now beginning to warm the vehicle's interior. Meanwhile, the windshield was doing its best to fog over.

Hannah hated being cold, which was why their apartment at The Dean was always a balmy 74 degrees. She was sure to be grumpy when he showed up at her work driving an icebox on wheels. But then again, when *wasn't* she grumpy these days?

Hank certainly wasn't going to sweat it. If she was cold, she was cold. That was life in Grimwood. Deal with it.

Still, once he pulled up to the curb in front of her office building, he went ahead and bumped the heat to the max in a last-ditch effort to close the comfort gap. He cranked up the music to compensate for the noise of the fan, and distracted himself by watching the people streaming in and out of the building. The majority of the passersby were smiling, which made him think not everyone at the company was as miserable working there as his girlfriend might lead him to believe.

Not that he put much stock in Hannah's complaining. He'd long suspected her dissatisfaction with her co-op had less to do with the job itself than it did with her major in general. He wondered if pinpointing her passion so early had left her feeling locked into a field that wasn't quite as romantic as she'd imagined it to be. It was one thing to be the self-professed architecture geek from middle school onward. It was something else entirely to dive into the actual nuts and bolts of the field and learn that true genius often comes with quite a few character flaws. While Frank Lloyd Wright's buildings were inspiring, Hank imagined the man himself was no picnic to deal with. He'd seen the pictures, the guy wore a *cape*. That sort of attire was telling.

Hank glanced at his watch and looked up, catching sight of a willowy blond in a formfitting winter coat and tight jeans. He did a double-take, certain for one fleeting moment that it was Rachel from the radio station. On closer look, he realized it wasn't her, but that brief moment of mistaken recognition had quickened his pulse. The rush was immediately followed by a sinking sense of guilt as Hannah emerged from the building and started his way. It wasn't that there was anything for him to feel guilty *about*. Nothing nefarious was going on. He'd worked a few more shifts with Rachel, and while there was nothing happening that he would call flirtatious, there *were* signs that all was not, perhaps, as it should be.

He enjoyed working with her though. Her enthusiasm was refreshing. She was excited to learn how the station ran. She loved music and the production program. It was the sort of intoxicating enthusiasm Jason had also given off when they were working at the station together. Of course, the added element of danger in this case was the fact that Rachel happened to be a very attractive, very *single* freshman girl, one who seemed to make a point of announcing her availability in increasingly emphasized ways. Any discussion of weekend plans included the clarification that she would just be hanging out with her 'girlfriends.' Any mention of a previous relationship was accompanied by an all but underlined disclaimer that said adventure had taken place with her *'ex'* boyfriend. In Hank's experience, no one ever used the term "ex" with such frequency, unless they wanted someone in the room to be aware of their current state of singledom. Since the only person in the room at those times was Hank, he found those moments both intriguing and dangerous.

"Hey."

The passenger door opened and Hannah plopped down beside him.

Hank leaned over to give her a kiss, but she was busy rummaging through her bag. She seemed irritated.

"How was your day?" he asked.

"Eh."

Hank gripped the steering wheel and waited for Hannah to fasten her seatbelt, then he stepped on the gas, just a little harder than necessary. The tires squealed slightly as he pulled away from the curb.

The jolt of acceleration caught Hannah's attention, briefly tugging her away from her current state of agitation. "Something wrong?"

Hank clenched his jaw. "Nah."

After a block of silence, Hannah seemed to tune into her surroundings.

"I'm starving," she sighed. "Are we going to dinner before or after the movie?"

"After. We can get some popcorn if you want."

"Yeah, I think I'll need it."

"What are we seeing again?"

Hank shrugged. "I forget. Something Loren picked out."

"Hmm…"

They drove the rest of the way to the theater in silence.

~

Hank and Braden slipped to the side of the theater lobby as the girls circled the wagons at the snack counter, comparing notes on the movie as they waited for their food.

Hank was just glad for the break. He stood with his hands in his pockets and his back pressed against the wall, slowly opening and closing his eyes in exhaustion. Now and then he looked up and surveyed the crowd milling around the room, noticing the couples specifically, and wondering what was going on behind the scenes in each of their relationships. Was *anyone* there as happy as they appeared to be?

Braden eyed Hank warily. "How are things going?"

"Eh, you know…"

Braden didn't actually, but his friend's tone told him all was not well.

"How about you?" Hank asked.

"I'm great," Braden said matter-of-factly.

The certainty of his answer caught Hank by surprise. He never really thought of Braden leaning more one way than the other. He was mister down the middle, productive as a robot and resistant to drama. What could possibly be going on in Braden's life to make him say 'great?'

The thought was still very much on Hank's mind as they filed into the theater and took their seats. He and Hannah slipped in first. Elissa and Brooke next. Then Loren and Braden at the end. For all intents and purposes, everyone appeared to be acting the same as always. Hannah and Elissa were arguing about something in the architecture program. Brooke and Loren were talking casually. And Braden was sitting at the end of the row, taking a sip from his drink, which he then set in the cup holder between his seat and Loren's. That seemed normal enough until Loren turned – without comment – took a sip of Braden's drink, and returned to her conversation.

Hank's eyes narrowed.

A short time later, when Loren casually reached over and squeezed Braden's leg above the knee, Hank knew for certain that something had finally changed between them.

~

After the show, they walked down the street to Brick's to grab a bite to eat. Hannah had enjoyed the movie. She reached down and took Hank's hand as they strolled down The Ave.

Hank was still observing Braden and Loren, watching for tells.

They got to Brick's and took their customary spots. No one needed to look at the menus. Betty came by with their drinks and took their orders; when she left, Loren turned and whispered something in Braden's ear. He looked up and smiled.

Suddenly, unable to control his curiosity a moment longer, Hank blurted out, "So, is something going on with you two or what?"

The table when silent.

Elissa and Brooke looked up.

Hannah turned and stared at him.

And Loren and Braden sat in dazed silence.

Braden played dumb, pointing back and forth between himself and Loren. "Is something going on between… who? Us?"

"Something, how?" Loren asked.

Braden scanned the table. "*Something* is kind of a… vague term. I don't-"

"Cut the shit you two," Hank interrupted. "Are you finally together or not?"

Loren looked at Brooke, who was doing her best to maintain a poker face. Then she met Braden's gaze and broke.

"We are," she admitted.

"I knew it!" Elissa said.

Brooke spun to face her girlfriend. "*You* knew?" Then to Loren, "I didn't say a word, I swear."

"Wait a minute!" Elissa said to Brooke. "*You* knew and you didn't tell me?

"I was committed to secrecy!" Brooke said. "And apparently you didn't need me to tell you, anyway. How did *you* find out?"

Elissa nodded at Braden. "Don Juan has been leaving his sneakers in the front hall for weeks. I kept spotting them as I was heading out the door for work."

Brooke seemed begrudgingly impressed. "OK, that's some good detective work." She brought her hand to her chin and addressed Loren and Braden in the manner of a stern librarian.

"OK, well, we've all been waiting three years for it. Let's get it over with."

Loren blushed, then she leaned forward and gave Braden a gentle kiss.

The group voiced their approval.

Under the table, Hannah squeezed Hank's hand.

4.

LOREN WOKE IN A daze, brewed a pot of coffee, and went about her morning routine, knocking back caffeine in an effort to clear the cobwebs from her mind. She was sitting at the counter, holding the warm mug in her hands, when she noticed the latest printout of Braden's novel. She hesitated, setting her drink down and approaching the manuscript like an idol in an Aztec ruin, afraid a sudden move might trigger a trap. Finally, after summoning the nerve to flip through the pages, she realized Braden had taken most, if not all of her suggestions from the previous draft. Subtle character and plot adjustments, revisions of sentences, and little tweaks she thought might add humor. They were all there in the reworked manuscript. She didn't know how much time went by. Minutes. Hours. It didn't matter. But once she'd finished reading through the draft, she felt, oddly as though she and Braden had entered into a new phase of their relationship. He took her seriously. He took her thoughts on his writing seriously. She knew that he was working on something new, something she hadn't seen yet, but knowing that he'd acted on her suggestions was surprisingly satisfying.

She gathered the pages together, gently tapped them on the edge of the counter, and set them back where she had found them. Then she took her coffee and set to work on her own writing for the remainder of the afternoon. Finally, after a long stretch of uncertainty, she was starting to see a through line, her time at Grimwood was beginning to make sense.

***

The pages flashed in Loren's mind a few days later as she sat beside Braden in class, listening to Professor Murch discussing the importance of revision and the value of finding an editor with a complementary eye.

"You can follow whatever theory you like, but for me, the hardest part is getting something down on the page. Once you have material to work with, it can only get better from there. Unless of course you over work it, in which case, the danger is that it seizes up and dies. That's where a good editor comes in. Someone who knows your work and knows when to stop tinkering is invaluable."

"The best editors are collaborators. They're not imposing their vision on your writing, but they're able to see where you're going, what you're aiming for, and where a little light and a touch of shade will set off the contours of your story. If you're lucky enough to find the right editor, it's like finding the perfect creative partner."

Loren watched Braden from the corner of her eye as he chewed on the end of his pen and absorbed the professor's advice.

"Another thing," Murch continued. "Writing is a lonely pursuit. Therefore, when you reach a milestone, a finished book or even the latest draft, it's important to celebrate the moment. Mark the occasion and replenish your reserves, because soon enough you'll be back at your desk, alone with the words."

Sitting at the keyboard, gathering thoughts and ideas, and trying to assemble them in an interesting and involving way *was* a lonely endeavor, and no doubt part of the reason Loren had found it so hard to write for the last couple of years. Of course, there were moments that made her think a better way was possible. Working on *Dead Men Don't* had been tremendously fun while it lasted. Even if their collaboration's unfortunate end had haunted her ever since, she would jump at the chance to try it again one day.

* * *

Brooke was chilled with dried sweat by the time she got back from crew practice. Elissa was just slipping out the door as she arrived home. They kissed in the hallway, two ships passing in the early morning.

"Why didn't you shower there?" Elissa asked.

"I was hoping to have breakfast with you before work, but the workout went longer than usual. I ran straight here to see if I could catch you."

"Oh, that's sweet. I'm sorry I can't stay. If it makes you feel any better, we wouldn't have the place to ourselves anyway."

"Is he here *again?*" Brooke asked.

"That he is," Elissa said as she started for the stairs. "I'll see you tonight though. Maybe we can go someplace for dinner."

"That would be nice."

Brooke could hear the murmur of the TV from around the corner as she entered the apartment. The bathroom door was ajar, with steam billowing through the opening as she padded into the living room.

Braden was watching TV. He was dressed in boxers, one sock, and what appeared to be Loren's bathrobe.

"How was practice?" he asked.

"Good," Brooke replied as she walked into the kitchen and pulled out a cereal bowl. She searched through the cabinets for her Lucky Charms, only to the find the box open and resting on the counter. For the amount of time Braden was spending at their apartment these days, Loren wasn't buying enough food for the two of them. Brooke filled her bowl and opened the fridge to discover there was barely enough milk for her cereal.

"Has Loren been in the shower for a while?"

"Maybe ten minutes? I'm sure she's almost done."

Brooke ate her breakfast and watched the weather guy rubbing guacamole on his face as part of a skincare segment. While it was nice to see Loren and Braden together, and it was good Braden was feeling comfortable at their apartment, she wondered if he wasn't perhaps feeling *too* at home there. It might be time she and Elissa nudged them to spend a few more nights at Braden's place once in a while. Brooke took another bite of cereal as she considered saying something, but lost her train of thought when the weather guy scraped a handful of green goo from his face and ate it.

"You're a smart guy, Braden. How can you watch this shit?"

"My brain is still waking up. Don't you guys have any coffee?"

Brooke took a deep breath – tempted to let him have it – but opted to take the high road and trudged off to her room instead.

"I think you lost a sock, Braden," Brooke said over her shoulder as she closed the door.

* * *

"Why the sudden interest in the gym?" Hank asked Braden as they entered the campus fitness center.

Braden held a hand on his stomach. "I'm feeling a little thick around the middle," he replied.

"Yeah, that seems to happen at the start of a relationship."

"So I've been told."

"What do you want to do? We can run the indoor track, use the treadmills, maybe work in some weights?"

"Whatever your routine is," Braden said. "You call the shots."

Hank led the way to the free weights. "We'll start here I think."

"How are things going?" Braden asked as they set to work.

Hank hoisted a dumbbell and grimaced at the question. "Eh, up and down."

"With school?"

"Not really."

"Work?"

"No." Hank shook his head, then stopped to think. "Well…"

"How are you and Hannah doing?"

" Eh… We're arguing a lot lately."

"That happens though, right?"

"I don't know, this feels different. She's been pretty miserable since she started the co-op. She wasn't liking her major before, but now she's like this dark cloud that drifts home at the end of the day. It sucks actually."

"Do you think things will get better when the co-op is finished?"

"I don't know. She'll still be working toward a degree that she doesn't seem to want anymore."

"I'm sorry to hear that," Braden said. Then something occurred to him. "Wait a minute. What's happening with your work?"

"What do you mean?"

"You hesitated when I asked about work."

"Eh you know, there's just-"

"Just… what? Which place are we talking about, Red Tomato or the station?"

"There's this… girl. At the station."

Braden set his weight down. "What did you do, Hank?"

"I didn't do anything. Relax."

"Who's this girl?"

"She's a freshman in the production program who started working the late shifts this fall. She's really cute, and *fun*, which believe me, is a nice change of pace these days. Nothing has happened, but it's making me rethink some things."

"Dammit. You and Hannah are supposed to be the couple that meets freshman year and spends the rest of their lives together."

"Maybe so. I mean, that's what I always thought-" Hank was getting a little defensive. "But I don't know. I want to be sure we're together because we *want* to be, and not because we're after some imaginary longevity award. That's no reason to stay with someone if things aren't working. You and Loren are still at that part of the relationship where you're having all those firsts. Hannah and I are in this sort of long *shitty* stretch."

"What do you mean firsts?"

"You know, like the first time you talk until dawn. First all night sex. The first time you have a huge fight and make up. Believe me, when those run out, things can really start to suck sometimes."

"Maybe this is just another first for you guys. The first time things start to cool off and reality barges in."

"Maybe… but it's feeling like something more."

"Well, ok then, you might as well tell me about this girl you're daydreaming about. What's her name?"

"Rachel."

"Rachel…" Braden repeated. "I don't like it."

"Would you shut up. This is all just a… thing."

"But you like her?"

"Yeah," Hank admitted. "I do."

"Well, shit."

* * *

Braden lay in bed beside Loren, drumming his fingers on his chest as he looked around her room and tried to catch his breath.

"So… I was talking to Hank today."

"Ah." Loren rolled over and looked him in the eyes. "Just what every girl dreams of hearing after making love."

"He said we're in that period with all the firsts."

"Well, what we just did wasn't really a first, but it was nice."

"I don't mean right *now*-"

"What was he talking about?"

Braden startled rattling them off. "You know, like the first fight."

"That was *years* ago," Loren countered as she slipped out of bed and pulled on a robe.

"First time making up."

"Ongoing."

"First weekend together."

"That's done too."

Braden raised an eyebrow. "First all night sex."

"That may be in progress. But first, I need some food, you want anything?"

"*Is* there anything?"

"Maybe not. We probably ought to make our first grocery store trip together."

She stopped at the doorway. "Why was Hank talking about that stuff in the first place?"

Braden hesitated, wondering if he'd said too much. He didn't want to keep something from her, but he also didn't want to betray Hank's confidence.

"I don't remember exactly."

Loren gave him a look. "Yeah, OK, Braden," she said as she headed for the kitchen.

5.

LOREN HAD JUST FINISHED ringing out a customer at the upstairs register when she heard a familiar voice behind her.

"Hey, Loren."

She turned to see Cole Phillips was standing in the office doorway.

"Cole. When did you get back?"

"I'm not back," he said. "Just home for Thanksgiving."

"Where are you living?"

"Well, I've been in London for a while now, but I'm thinking of heading to Paris when I fly back."

"Well *that* sounds nice. Are you there for work?"

He hesitated a split second before he answered. "School."

The word came out like an uncertain question, which, paired with that moment of uncertainty, told Loren everything she needed to know. He was doing the same thing he'd always done, he'd just found a way to do it in more exotic locales.

"I see it's getting busy around here," he observed.

"Yeah, it seems to start earlier every year."

"How is Braden?"

"Braden?" she didn't know if Cole knew about the two of them or not. "I think he's doing OK."

Cole nodded in a way that still left her wondering. Was it instinctive, or did he know there were things she wouldn't share with him now? Did it even matter?

"Do you have plans for Thanksgiving?"

"We're having everybody over to our place for dinner," Loren replied. "*We* as in me, Brooke, and Elissa."

"Oh. I figured you'd be at what's her name's place again."

Cathie Pepper.

Loren suddenly realized they hadn't invited her yet.

"No. We thought we'd host this year. What about you?"

"The usual. Mom and Dad and the usual assortment of friends and business relations."

"Oh, that should be… fun?" She laughed in spite of herself, and for the first time the tension eased.

Cole smiled. "Yeah. Board meetings as family holidays. Bet you miss that, right?"

"Yeah, good times," Loren said as she brushed her fingers through her hair. "Well, I hope for your sake it goes well."

"Thanks." He smiled and looked at his watch. "I probably better hit the road."

"Happy Thanksgiving," she said. "Have fun in Paris."

They shared a quick hug, then Cole started down the stairs.

~

"So, Cole stopped by the store today."

Brooke looked up from her books. *"Really?* And how did that go?"

"Well, we didn't talk long, but it was actually kind of nice."

"Does he know about you and-"

"I don't think so."

"Things might get awkward when he finds that out."

"I don't know that it even matters," Loren said. "Besides, it's not like our paths will be crossing again anytime soon. He's off living the good life in Europe."

"Some folks have all the hard luck, don't they?"

"He did bring up one thing I hadn't thought about."

"What's that?"

"He figured we'd be having Thanksgiving at Cathie Pepper's place again. We should probably invite her."

"I've been thinking the same thing." Brooke said as she walked into the kitchen. "To be honest, it's been bothering me. I was expecting an invite by now, but when I didn't hear anything from her, I thought it might be fun to host it here. Better that than risking Thanksgiving at Hank and Hannah's place and having someone get beaten to death with a frozen turkey."

"In their defense, I don't think they're a danger to themselves or others. Not yet, anyway. Plus, Hannah would never forget to defrost the turkey."

Brooke filled a kettle and put it on the stove. "I don't know, Loren. They're getting *pretty* dysfunctional. Elissa and I had lunch with them last week. It wasn't pleasant. Thirty minutes around all that bickering and I thought I was developing an ulcer."

"I'm sure finals aren't helping either," Loren said.

"They can't be helping *anyone* right now. At any rate, I'll give Cathie a call after my test tomorrow."

* * *

"Do you ever think Charlie Brown's problems are self-inflicted?" Brooke asked Elissa as they set the table for dinner. The TV was tuned to the Thanksgiving parade, where America's favorite blockhead was just drifting into view.

"Totally. The power and peril of self-fulfilling prophesies. I've always liked Snoopy. That is one self-actualizing dog."

Loren and Braden were stretched out on the couch. "I've got a question," Loren said. "Is Woodstock a boy or a girl?"

"I think Woodstock's a girl," Brooke said.

"I'm not one for labels," Elissa replied. "But I remember reading somewhere that Charles Schulz started out thinking Woodstock was a girl, but at some point he made him a boy."

"Why are we watching the parade now anyway?" Braden asked. "Didn't this happen like six hours ago?" He reached over and picked up the remote, only for Brooke to step between him and the television.

"Don't you *dare*. We are watching the parade because I recorded the parade and I *always* watch the parade. It's not Thanksgiving until *this* New Yorker has seen every Macy's-subsidized minute."

"I just thought maybe we could watch football or something."

"Since when do you care about football?" Loren asked.

"Isn't that what people do on Thanksgiving? Watch football?"

"No," Brooke snapped. "They watch the parade. Now put that remote *down*."

Braden looked around the room uncertainly. He couldn't tell if Brooke was joking. "OK. OK. I'll put it down."

"Thank you," Brooke said as she returned to setting the table.

Hank and Hannah were in the kitchen. Judging from the sounds of their conversation, the two of them were still clashing. The rest of the group exchanged uncomfortable looks.

"Did you ever hear anything from Cathie Pepper?" Loren asked.

Brooke shook her head. "Nope. I left her a few messages, and I went by the house twice, but the place was dark."

"Maybe she's with family?" Braden suggested.

"As far as I knew, she and Jason were basically the only family she had."

"That's weird," Loren said. "I hope everything is all right."

Hank and Hannah emerged from the kitchen, seemingly through the worst of their latest skirmish. Hannah took a seat on the arm of the couch.

"Anyone want a beer?" Hank asked from the kitchen.

"I'll take one." Braden said as he got to his feet and joined him.

Hank popped open a bottle of Genesee and handed it to Braden, who took a sip and peeked around the corner. Hannah was talking with the girls as the parade coverage cut to a commercial break.

"So are things going any better?" Braden asked Hank.

"Ups and downs. I'm still hoping things turn around when she starts up classes again."

"You think that will make a difference?"

"I hope so, man. What else can I do?"

"Whatever happened with that girl at the station?"

"Rachel?" Hank dropped his voice. "Nothing has happened, but…"

"But what?

Hank took a sip of his drink and gathered his thoughts together. "Let's just say she's still very much on my mind, but I'm trying like hell to keep my thoughts straight. She invited me to a party she and the people on her floor are throwing in a couple of weeks."

"What are you going to do?" Braden asked.

"What am I supposed to do?! I have a girlfriend. I can't be going to some party by myself."

"Wouldn't you sort of be going with Rachel?"

"Yeah," I guess so.

"Has Hannah met this girl?"

"Of course not! Hannah has no idea she even exists."

"What do you want to do?"

"I just want to have fun. I mean, I love Hannah, I don't want to fuck that up. But I can't get this other girl out of my head. It's driving me crazy."

"Is there any way to just not think about it?"

"Sure," Hank said as he lifted his drink. "That's what this is for."

~

Braden and Loren lay in her bed together recapping the evening.

"Hank and Hannah seem to be doing better," Loren said.

"You think so? I don't know."

"No?"

He looked at her.

"Do you know something?" she asked.

"I think he may be having some doubts."

"Oh. And here I was thinking they seemed less tense."

"Who knows. Something can always change. He's hoping things blow over once she's done with her co-op."

"That's a strange thing to pin his hopes on."

The two of them were quiet again.

"Speaking of tension," Braden said. "Am I imagining things, or do I seem to be getting on Brooke's nerves recently?"

"Maybe. I guess we *have* been spending a lot of time over here."

"Think we should try my place for a while?"

"That might not be a bad idea. I'll bring some extra clothes over this weekend."

***

Loren moved in over Thanksgiving break. As she made a point of explaining, she was still living with Brooke and Elissa, but the bulk of her clothes and personal items were slowly migrating to Braden's building a few blocks away. They quickly fell into a routine of classes, work, and evenings spent together. There were periods in which Braden was writing, and she was writing. And there were times he slipped away to the library to immerse himself in his projects, while Loren did the same at the apartment

They read together. They discussed their days. They prepared meals. And they made love. All in all, they were ensconced in a bubble of domestic bliss, save for one incident a week after Loren moved in.

Fortunately, it didn't happen in Braden's apartment, but it was close enough to give them a scare. They knew almost nothing about the woman involved, save for the fact that her name was Harper, she appeared to be in her late-forties, and she was always complaining of a headache when they said hello to her in passing. Her distinguishing characteristics were her eternally bloodshot eyes and a staggered gait. Loren thought she had a drinking problem. Braden diagnosed her as nuts.

One thing was certain, Harper had an ill-advised habit of throwing food in the oven while she took a shower after her late-shifts at work. Apparently, she'd been doing this for years, but it wasn't until the week after Loren moved in that their neighbor forgot she had a meal in the oven and went straight to sleep after her shower. As Harper slept, her Stouffer's stuffed peppers grew toasty, then blistered, then they burst into flames. Thankfully, the building's fire alarms went off in time. The residents of the building, Braden and Loren included, evacuated to safety, and Harper awoke and made it out of the building unscathed. Her dinner and her apartment were not as lucky.

After the smoke and firetrucks cleared out, Harper was sent away without explanation. Though she and Braden were fine, Loren noticed Braden's stacks of papers, including his manuscripts, soon vanished from sight. She didn't know if he was keeping them in the building, or if he'd found a safe space off-site, but Loren suspected the incident had spooked him.

Otherwise, aside from that one incident, life at the moment was very sweet indeed.

~

Things were not good.

Hank and Hannah had all but stopped speaking. She was at an all-time low point, and his empathy had run dry. Most mornings, she either left before he was up, or they exchanged a few terse comments about the day ahead before he dropped her off at work and headed to Red Tomato for a shift, where he would inevitably sneak at least one more beer than felt wise.

His nights at the station certainly didn't help things. Hank couldn't recall the last time he'd felt such a guilty sense of excitement, but the anticipation of seeing Rachel while working a late shift was only making matters worse. He went about his duties, he nodded along and hit his marks, but all the while, his eyes were drifting, and his imagination was running wild. What's more, he had the distinct feeling that he was being reeled in, slowly but surely; it happened so smoothly that he couldn't pinpoint the moment when he'd swallowed the hook.

The Saturday after Thanksgiving, Howard called at the last moment to see if Hank could cover a few extra hours at the station. It was midday, a time he'd never actually worked before, but considering the tension at home, and a general wish to get out of the apartment, Hank readily agreed to head up the hill and get on the air.

Hank was seated in the booth, introducing a slate of songs, when he looked through the glass and saw Rachel strolling down the empty corridor. She was wearing a bright white cap with an oversized pompom on the top. Her cheeks were flush from the cold outside. After he finished his on-air shpiel, Hank cut the mic and stepped out into the hall. The two of them were the only people in the building.

"What are you doing here?"

Rachel held up an envelope. "Just picking up my paycheck for some holiday shopping."

"How was your Thanksgiving?"

She shrugged. "You know. It was OK."

"You didn't go home to-?" He couldn't recall where she was from, but he knew it was somewhere in California.

"Sacramento? No, I wanted to try to save some money since I'll just be flying back again next month."

"Oh yeah. Christmas is coming up quick."

"Yes it is."

Hank couldn't be sure, but while the flush seemed to be washing out of Rachel's cheeks, his own face was feeling warmer by the second.

"So, Hank," Rachel began, her eyes tilting to look up at him. "Do you think you can make it to that party I was telling you about?"

"I'm not sure if I can."

"What do I need to do to convince you?"

"Trust me, I *want* to go. I just don't know if I should."

"It's just a party…" she whispered conspiratorially.

Hank mumbled something in response as Rachel stepped in closer. The next thing he knew, her lips were on his neck, and his fingers were in her hair. The rest was a blur as they fumbled toward the dilapidated couch in the hallway, falling onto the burst cushions, and kissing passionately. They went on that way for a while until the radio hit dead air.

"Hank…" Rachel murmured.

"-What?"

"The music stopped."

Hank jumped to his feet and hurried back to the booth.

His heart was pounding as he sat down at the microphone and hit the broadcast button. "How about that one, folks?" he said, trying like hell to recall which song had just ended.

Rachel leaned in the open doorway, flashing a seductive smile that only further scrambled his thoughts as he struggled to form a complete sentence.

"Think about that party," she whispered before she closed the door and slipped away.

* * *

Hannah had a tendency to retrench when she was miserable. She knew she did it, and she knew it pushed people away, but in the depths of despair, she couldn't help herself. When she was kid, she could get away with it, because her father, for all his strengths as a parent, was a uniquely unhappy man, one who had his own ways of walling himself off from the world, as well as from his daughter. You could say, in a sense that she'd learned from the best.

Yet, when it comes to endings, even the most cynical malcontents are susceptible to nostalgia. It's easy to view a place or situation in a softer light when you know for certain you are *never* going back that way again. So it was on Hannah's last day on the job. As she cleaned out her workspace, she found herself halfway excited for the going away party after work, and wishing she'd told Hank about it.

Later that night, after the second round of drinks, Hannah was feeling reflective. She sat in the warmth of the Mexican restaurant with her soon to be former coworkers, looking out at the street as the margaritas went to work on her synapses. The temperature was plunging, and there were flurries in the air. Her mind was a jumble, but in an instant, one unmistakable fact sliced through the haze.

She was fucking things up at home; pushing her luck with Hank by fixating on her problems, and failing to appreciate what the two of them had going. Which was a lot.

It was too late to make plans now. Hank was working another late-shift at the station, but by the time he signed off that night, Hannah was determined to be waiting outside for him in the falling snow, where she would promise to make things right.

~

Hank fumbled with the lock as he tried to close the station's front door. Rachel leaned in closer, pulling tight on his shoulder as she kissed him. He'd arrived at work determined not to do this again. The guilt was overwhelming, but the excitement when they were alone was every bit as powerful. And so, it continued; the night spent rushing through song introductions, loading up the playlists so the two of them could make out on the floor behind the desk, out of sight from any unexpected visitors who might stop by the station.

"My floor is having that party tonight," Rachel whispered. "Will you come?"

A shiver ran up Hank's spine.

Once he went there – and alcohol and Rachel's bedroom were added to the equation – he knew what the result would be; a line would be crossed, and there would be no coming back.

Rachel slid her fingers down the front of his shirt and kissed him on the neck.

"Yeah, let's go," Hank said.

The storm had picked up by the time Hank finished his broadcast and switched over to *The Best of Howard Lester.* He and Rachel pulled on their heavy coats and headed out for the night. Snow billowed around them as they stepped outside. Rachel leaned in close as he locked the door.

"Hurry up so we can get to that party," she said flirtatiously.

"Trust me, I'm trying," Hank said as he snuck another kiss and pulled on the handle. "I'm just trying to avoid disaster…"

It was then that he turned around and saw Hannah standing in the shadows. She looked at him for a moment, cocking her head to the side – slightly tipsy – but more hurt than angry.

Hank stared back at her, at a complete loss.

Hannah was the first to find her words.

"Listen, Hank. You don't owe me anything, and I don't owe you anything."

He looked from Hannah to Rachel, who was standing with one hand held over her mouth. Stunned.

Hannah hurried away, cutting across the field between the Student Union and the President's Mansion.

"Hannah, wait!" He turned to Rachel. "I'm afraid you're gonna have to go to that party by yourself."

Hank took off running after Hannah as she disappeared around the corner of the building. She was heading back to The Avenue, but getting there by way of the old stairs.

The pathway was icy and the snow was blowing in at a disorienting angle, making it hard for him to see where he was going.

"Hannah!" Hank shouted as he came around the corner, emerging at the top of the concrete steps. He hadn't been this way since Jason's accident freshman year.

His stomach tightened.

His feet slipped on the icy pavement as he looked down the stairs.

Hannah was just stepping off the curb on the street down below.

She'd made it down safely.

Hank squeezed the railing in his bare hand, feeling the cold in the joints of his fingers as he debated whether to follow after her or go around the long way.

Against his better judgment, he started down the stairs, holding the rail in a vice grip as he made his way down the snowy, worn stairs. With each footfall, he thought of Jason, and imagined him walking down these same steps.

Hank could see how it had happened. Water seemed to drain down these stairs, encasing them in a frozen glaze. There were no lights. And the treads were each just a hair too shallow, causing anyone who went down them to rest unsteadily on the back of their heels.

He paused at the landing near the halfway point, feeling the tension in his arms and shoulders. He'd crossed an invisible line with Rachel, so perhaps he deserved this.

Two steps from the bottom, he had a sudden, vivid vision of Jason sprawled out on the snow, crimson blooming from his head.

Hank stepped to the sidewalk and the image disappeared. He moved through the darkness that lingered over the sidewalk as the knot in his stomach uncoiled. As Hank looked the way he had come, there in the shadows, just for an instant, he thought he saw a familiar figure standing in silhouette. Then it was gone.

~

He trudged up the stairs at the apartment, dreading the confrontation that was sure to come the moment he walked in the front door. But when he opened the front door, he was met by only silence. The light in the front hall was on. Hannah's shoes were set neatly on the floor.

The door to their bedroom was closed. The light was off.

When he walked into the living room, he found his pillow and a blanket tossed on the couch.

~

Hank woke with a start, his eyes immediately going to the bedroom door. It was open. Hannah was gone.

An hour later, he was sitting at the counter in Braden's place, drinking coffee as Braden and Loren made breakfast in their pajamas.

"It was like Jason was standing right there in the darkness, just for a split second," Hank said as he looked down at his coffee. "I must be cracking up."

Braden caught Loren's eye.

"I fucked everything up. The minute I saw those stairs, I realized how I would feel if something happened. I've been taking Hannah for granted. She's been so unhappy, but I could have been more understanding."

"You said yourself she's been miserable to live with though," Braden observed.

"So what are you saying, Braden?" Loren asked. "Misery is an excuse to start screwing around with some freshman girl?"

"Well, no…"

"You're right," Loren said to Hank as she dropped a plate of eggs in front of him. "You did fuck everything up. I just hope you can fix it."

~

"It's my fault," Hannah said as she lay face down on Brooke and Elissa's couch.

Brooke sat beside her, rubbing her hand on her back. "No it's not. How are you at fault in this scenario? Freshman girls are bad news."

"Well, now wait a minute," Elissa added as she walked past with a mug of coffee. "Let's not go pinning the blame on the girl here."

"Why not?" Brooke asked.

"It takes two to tango, Elissa said. "And it sounds like Hank all but had a rose in his teeth."

Hannah sat up. "You're making him sound like Pepe Le Pew."

"Nothing wrong with that," Brooke replied. "What he did stinks. You didn't do anything wrong here…"

"*Yeah…*" Elissa jumped in again, "but you sort of did."

Brooke's shot her girlfriend a wide-eyed '*what the hell?*' expression.

"You said it yourself, you've been hating your co-op, you *hate* your major, and you've been taking it all out on Hank."

"That's still not an excuse-"

Hannah cut Brooke off. "No, Elissa's right. I've been taking things for granted."

Elissa continued. "I have a friend in Tacoma who has a saying, 'Make your own money, marry someone funny.'"

Brooke looked from Elissa to Hannah and back to Elissa. "I'm suddenly dating Mr. Miyagi. What in the world does that mean?"

Elissa shrugged. "I don't know. But I've always taken it to mean you've got to make your own luck. You do you. Money, happiness, whatever it is that keeps you going and gives you some purpose, that's on *you* to figure out. You can't expect the person you're with to deliver all the goods, you just need to find someone to help ease the burden. So maybe Hank wasn't quite meeting his side of the bargain, but it sounds like you haven't been giving him much reason to try either."

"Shit." Hannah sighed. "I think you're right."

~

Hank was at the apartment when she got back. Hannah could hear him putting dishes away as she entered. The sounds in the kitchen stopped the moment he heard the front door shut. The floorboards creaked as he walked around the corner to greet her.

"Hey," Hank murmured.

"Hey."

"I am so sorry about what happened."

She just shook her head.

"And nothing else happened!" Hank explained. "We kissed, that's it."

"It doesn't matter." Hannah continued to shake her head. "It's OK.

Hank's whole face relaxed. "It is?"

She stepped toward him.

He bit his lower lip.

"Are we good then?"

"We're fine."

"It will *never* happen again," Hank said "I promise."

She straightened up. "You don't have to do that Hank. There's clearly something wrong here."

Hank's face fell as the bottom dropped out of his stomach. "What do you mean?"

"There's no question that I haven't been happy. Not for a long time. And I certainly can't blame you for what that's done to our relationship."

"So what are you saying? You want to end this?"

"I don't know, Hank. But I need to figure some things out. And maybe you do, too. Because whatever this is, and whatever is going on, I think we both need to get it out of our systems."

Hank stood there, frozen, his shoulders slumped as he looked around the apartment. "I guess I'll start looking for a place."

"You don't have to. You can stay here. I already worked things out with Brooke and Elissa. With Loren basically living with Braden these days, I'm going to move into her room and stay with them for a while."

"Oh. So... that's it?"

"For now maybe. Let's just take some time."

"Have we broken up? Is this a break?"

"A break, broken, it doesn't matter. Whatever happens, we're going to be OK either way."

Hannah sidestepped him and headed into their bedroom, where she started opening drawers and pulling her clothes out in piles.

"What are you doing?"

"I'm going to pack my stuff up and bring it over there."

"Do you have to do it so *quickly?*" Hank pleaded.

"Why wait? If I'm going to move out, I might as well do it."

Hank watched her until an angry weight began to build in his stomach, then he turned and stormed out of the apartment.

~

Hank hung around the apartment the next day. It was one of the rare occasions when he didn't have work scheduled at either of his jobs, and it left him with an alarming lack of distraction.

He considered calling Hannah at the girls' apartment, but he was still alternating between despair and irritation. He wasn't feeling self-righteous – he was clearly in the wrong – but he couldn't come to terms with the way things had ended. Or if they'd actually *ended* at all.

He studied the apartment key Hannah had left on the table.

How could she act like everything was fine, yet still put their relationship on ice? Where did that leave them?

By Sunday night his thinking had switched gears. If things with Rachel had gotten him into this mess, why not dive in head first? For the first time that year, he walked to the residential side of campus. Consulting the slip of paper on which Rachel had written her dorm info, he went to her building, rode the elevator up to her floor, and was halfway to her room when he regained his senses and rode the lift back down.

He picked up a six pack on the way home, and was soon back in the apartment, flipping through the channels until he stopped on an episode of *Dr. Quinn Medicine Women*. As Jane Seymour dispensed cheerful medical care to the people of the great American prairie, Hank Pierce felt the darkness close in.

6.

HANK SIDESTEPPED LOREN AND Braden, who were kissing under the mistletoe as he walked in. This was the first time he'd been to Elissa, Brooke, and now Hannah's apartment. Technically, it was still Loren's place as well. Life was getting messy.

In honor of the season, garland and lights were draped around the living room. A thin tree sat in the corner, the top tipping downward under the weight of its star.

"I like the Dr. Seuss tree," Braden noted as he and Loren followed Hank into the living room.

"It does have a Seussian quality," Loren agreed. "Very nice ladies."

Hannah greeted Hank with an awkward hug. "Merry Christmas."

"Merry Christmas. I love what you've done with the place."

"Did you ever see what it looked like before?"

He laughed. "Nope. But I'm sure this tops it!"

"Brooke and Elissa did most of it, but I put my two cents in here and there…" Hannah glanced down at her drink. "Did you want some nog?"

"That would be great," Hank said as they headed for the kitchen.

The rest of the group watched Hank and Hannah from the sidelines, but no one commented.

"Anyone else feel like we were all *just* here?" Braden mused.

"What are you talking about?" Elissa said. "It feels like *you* were just here, but I haven't seen these other clowns in ages."

"I mean 'here' like weren't we all just preparing for the holidays like, yesterday?"

"Yeah, I feel the same way," Brooke said.

"What are you guys doing for the break?" Loren asked.

Elissa put her arm around Brooke. "We're staying here."

"What about you?" Braden asked Hannah as she returned with Hank in tow.

"I'm going back to Chicago."

"And I'll be in Albany," Hank said.

"What about you, Loren?" Brooke asked. "Are you going home to New Mexico?"

Loren's head shot up as she prepared to remind her that New Mexico and Colorado were *not* interchangeable, but she stopped short when she realized Brooke was teasing her again.

"Actually, I'm going to Long Island with Braden. We're spending Christmas with his father."

Brooke smiled. *"Reeeally?"*

"In theory anyway," Braden cautioned. "My old man has a poor track record when it comes to holiday appearances."

"For my sake, I hope he shows. Who am I supposed to talk to while you're buried in your writing every day?"

Braden shook his head. "That won't be a problem. I'm leaving my computer and everything here."

"Well that's news to me." Loren said. "Can we toast to that?"

"Absolutely," Elissa said.

They were all raising their glasses when they heard a knock at the door and turned to see Cathie Pepper standing in the front hall, a bag in her hands, and a nervous smile on her face.

"Hey, everybody. Sorry to barge in on you-"

~

"I'm sorry it took so long to get back to you," Cathie said once they'd caught up. "I've been traveling. I thought it might be good to get away from Grimwood for a while."

"Where did you go?" Hannah asked.

"A few of places. I spent a little time in the UK. A little time in Ireland. We went on a bike tour around the Ring of Kerry, which was a lot of fun."

"'*We?*'" Brooke noted. "Is there… anything you want to tell us?"

"Yeah, I met someone. *Finally* as Jason would have said." She smiled at Brooke. "He works at the hospital. His name is Luke."

"I'm so happy for you," Brooke said.

"Thank you. He's really great. And you guys…" she turned to Loren and Braden. "I'm *really* happy it's worked out. I'm happy for all of you. It makes all the difference to spend the holidays with someone special."

Elissa rubbed Brooke's back.

Hank and Hannah exchanged uncomfortable glances.

* * *

True to his word, Braden didn't bring any of his projects with him. The notebooks, the laptop, none of it came along for the ride. Now books, those were another matter, but he and Loren *both* stuffed their bags with things they wanted to finish reading over the break.

They set out early in Braden's old car, getting on the thruway right after breakfast, and driving almost nonstop until they'd passed the city and continued on to the Island. Once they were in Huntington, Braden made a few stops for essentials. First up was a trip through the drive thru Dairy Barn, a red, barn shaped convenience store that apparently specialized in the car-side delivery of any product derived from a cow.

"What are we here for?" Loren asked as they waited for someone to come up to their window.

"Eggnog of course."

"Of course."

"If you think of anything we need at the store, we'll stop at IGA down the street just as soon as we're done here."

"Couldn't we just get eggnog there too?"

"*No way.*" Braden gave her a perturbed look. "You buy eggnog at Dairy Barn."

"Well, all right then." Loren laughed. "That's good to know."

~

They passed a harbor and turned at an old post office. From there, they wound their way uphill, passing a squiggling side street – whimsically named 2 Rod Road – hooked a left on Bay Avenue, a right on Kaiser Hill, and quietly merged with Vineyard Road.

"I love the street names around here," Loren observed.

"Why's that?"

"They don't seem real. It's like they've been pulled from a storybook." Her eyes went wide as they turned into the driveway of an imposing three-story house. "Jesus, Braden, you grew up here?"

"I did," Braden said as he pulled to a stop behind an olive green Pinto.

"Is someone here?"

"Olga. You're going to love her."

Braden led the way to the back door, where he slipped a key into the old Yale, twisting it open as he reflexively pushed his foot against the kickplate where the door rubbed against the frame. He set their bags on the green marmoleum inside and beckoned for Loren to come in from the cold.

Loren looked around the kitchen, which, if she had to guess, hadn't been updated since the Eisenhower administration. Then she followed Braden into the dining room, where he pointed out a small hole in a stained glass window above the buffet.

"Pops did that with a **BB** gun when he was ten."

"How long has this house been in your family?"

"Forever."

The dining room led to a wide open living room, where two couches faced each other in front of a large fireplace. Around the corner, a piano held court in a parlor with thick red carpet that extended up a long, winding staircase that hugged the edge of the room and ascended to an open balcony overhead.

A door could be heard closing upstairs, followed by the quiet creaking of floorboards.

"Olga, is that you?"

"Who else would it be?" Olga said matter-of-factly as she emerged at the second-floor railing. "How was your trip?"

"Good."

"Is Mr. McNutt's old car still running?"

"So far so good," Braden said, knocking on the handrail at the bottom of the stairs.

Loren watched as the older woman made her way down the stairs, one slow step at a time.

"Your father called as I was making the beds." She motioned to a nearby phone desk. A red light was blinking on the answering machine. "He left you a message."

"Should I listen?"

Olga sighed and shook her head.

"You must be Loren," she said as she reached the ground floor.

Braden crossed the room and pressed the play button. His father's voice filled the background.

"I'm happy you're spending the holidays with my boy," Olga said.

"It's so nice to be here," Loren replied.

The two of them eavesdropped on David McNutt's convoluted explanation for his last minute need to stay overseas for the holiday. Loren watched Olga's eyebrows pinch together as the message continued.

Braden stopped the recording when his father began to wish them 'Merry Christmas.'

Olga locked Loren in her gaze. "David has never been good to that boy," she said softly.

Braden walked back to them. When he spoke again, his voice was just a hair louder than before, like he was trying to buck himself up. But it was clear he wasn't all that surprised. "I guess I should have seen that coming."

"His loss, right?" Olga said.

"Absolutely."

Loren sensed this was a familiar rejoinder in such circumstances.

"Well, I don't want to keep you two much longer," Olga said as she led the way to the kitchen. "Harry came by and brought the Christmas stuff up from the basement. The boxes are in the living room. I went ahead and stocked the fridge and freezer for you. Though if I had to guess, you've already stopped for eggnog and your 'essentials.'"

"Yes. I was shown the Dairy Barn," Loren said.

"Oy, Dairy Barn. His grandfather was the same way. You cannot get the eggnog and milk at Southdown or IGA, it *has* to be from the Dairy Barn. I could never taste the difference."

"There's a difference, trust me," Braden told Loren.

Olga threw up her hands. "Anyway, I put a few casseroles in the fridge. The reheating directions are taped on top."

"Thank you," Braden said.

"Don't thank me," Olga said. "I made them for Loren here. Make sure she gets her fair share."

Olga gave Braden a hug. "It's good to have you home. And Loren, it's a pleasure to meet you."

Loren watched from the window as Braden walked Olga to her car. It was clear observing the two of them that they'd known one another for a lifetime. Braden stood and waved as Olga's green car pulled out of the driveway. Though he looked slightly crestfallen as he turned around, his face brightened again when he saw Loren watching him.

~

Braden gave her the rest of the tour before dinner.

His grandfather's office sat on the second floor, just off of the main bedroom. Braden showed her the old desk, and the bookcase full of titles Pops had edited throughout his publishing career.

"This is only half of them," he said. "The rest are in the library upstairs."

Loren stood at the office window, looking out over Long Island Sound.

"It's beautiful," she said.

"Not as beautiful as you," Braden said as he stepped behind her and kissed her on the neck.

"No funny business, buddy," Loren teased. "I need to see this library first."

The library didn't disappoint. Shelf after shelf of hardbound classics and well-preserved first editions lined the walls.

Loren took down an original, hardcover copy of *The Wizard of Oz* and flipped through it carefully. "I always loved this book."

"It was one of Pops favorites as well." Braden pointed to the line-up of sixteen more Frank Baum originals. "He has them all."

Loren closed the book and returned it to the shelf. She walked over to Braden and kissed him. "Thank you for bringing me here. It's nice to see where you came from."

~

Braden built a fire and opened a bottle of red wine as the first of Olga's casseroles warmed in the oven. As they ate, he told Loren more about the house and shared some of his favorite memories from growing up there.

They sat in front of the fire after dinner, reading late into the night. At one point, after she'd closed her book, and for reasons she would never quite understand, a question popped into Loren's mind.

"What do you think about writers completing other authors books if they die before they're finished?"

Braden looked up as the fire crackled. "I'm all for it."

"Really? I'm surprised"

"Yeah, why not? Anything to get another book on the shelves."

"Are you joking?"

"No, I'm being serious. It's a shame to let someone's work go unread, I'd rather get it out there so their fans can see everything. And when another author takes over – assuming they're giving it their very best effort – it brings something extra to the table, like they're channeling the author from beyond the grave. It's creepy, but kind of… cool."

* * *

They spent the next day puttering around town, picking up odds and ends at the various shops and stores. Almost every place they stopped inspired a story about a time Braden had been there with his grandfather.

The Book Revue was a dangerous place for two booksellers and self-professed book addicts. By the time they rang out their selections, they'd each filled their baskets with books for themselves, books for each other, and gifts for the next day.

Snow was falling as they started for home, and by the time they reached the house, it was beginning to accumulate.

After taking some time to wrap his gifts, Braden set to work decorating the Christmas tree in the front parlor. Loren was still upstairs as Braden searched intently through the boxes of ornaments.

"Ah, there you are," he said as he extracted an old, yellowed box, carefully unfolded the top, and removed a silver ornament with a plug. When he connected the ornament to the tree's lights, it began emitting a warbling birdsong.

"What is that?" Loren called down the stairs.

"What?"

"That noise? It's like a chirping sound."

"Chirping?" Braden asked dumbly.

The noise continued as Loren emerged at the bottom of the stairs, her arms full of packages. "Seriously. What the hell is that?"

Braden held the ornament up proudly.

She gave him a blank stare.

"You *like* that?"

"It's fun."

Loren ignored him and began placing the wrapped gifts under the tree.

The chirping continued.

"OK, seriously, you're not going to leave that going all night, are you?"

Braden laughed. "No, it would drive me crazy too. I just like knowing it's on the tree."

He unplugged the ornament and the birdsong warbled down to nothing.

"Well, now I feel kind of bad," Loren admitted.

"Should I plug it back in?"

"*No.*" She stood back and admired the tree. "It's looking good. Let's see what other ornaments you and Pops have."

Outside, the snow continued to fall.

Inside, Braden and Loren decorated the tree.

They ate dinner and sipped wine by the fire.

As Christmas Eve drew to a close, they made love and huddled together under the covers, falling asleep in one another's arms as the house was blanketed in snow.

* * *

"Merry Christmas, Bedford Falls!" Elissa hollered as she ran down the middle of The Ave, slipping and sliding in the freshly fallen snow.

"Shhh!" Brooke said as she doubled over in laughter.

"*What?!*" Elissa shouted back.

"You're going to wake everyone up!"

"Who's here? Everyone is back home," Elissa said as she trudged back to Brooke. "It's just you and me, babe."

"Grimwood is beautiful when it snows."

A dusting of snowflakes had landed on Brooke's face and melted, the drops of water glistening in the moonlight. Elissa pulled off her mittens and brushed them away.

"I think *you're* beautiful when it snows," Elissa said.

Brooke smiled. "You are too."

They kissed.

"Let's go home," Brooke whispered.

"OK," Elissa said as they continued walking through the quiet, moonlit street. "Can I ask you something?"

"What?"

"Why didn't you go back to New York?"

"Because you were staying here," Brooke said. "I wanted to spend the holidays with you."

"Have you told your parents about me?" Elissa asked.

Brooke brushed a strand of hair from her eyes. "Yeah. I've talked about you"

"But have you *told* them about me. About us?"

"…Not yet."

"I'm not going to get mad or anything," Elissa said. "I'm just wondering, why haven't you? Is it the whole…"

Brooke shook her head. "It's not that. My parents are… difficult people."

"Did you ever tell them about Jason?"

"Yeah. They met him."

"Then what is it?"

"They barely gave Jason the time of day. I was protective of him. Just like I'm protective of you."

"But *everyone* loved Jason," Elissa said. "I never knew him and I feel like *I* love Jason."

Brooke reached over and took Elissa's hand. "I promise you, what my parent's think about anything doesn't matter to me. I just don't want them coloring our time together. I wanted to spend Christmas with you *here*, in our own little world."

"That's all I want too." Elissa said. Then she grinned. "I also kind of want to do that Merry Christmas Bedford Falls thing again too."

Brooke rolled her eyes. "I'd rather just go home, climb into bed, and watch the movie with you."

"That sounds good too."

***

"What's that sound," Hannah asked, straining her ears to identify what she was hearing on the other end of the phone line.

"My father and brother are having a ping pong championship," Hank said. "The Pierce Cup."

"Do you play in this?"

"Are you kidding? I'm the reigning champion," Hank exclaimed. "I've held the title for years."

"*Ping pong?* I just can't picture this."

"It's true."

"Henry," Hank's father called in the background. "You're on deck next."

"*Henry?!*" Hannah asked.

"What? That's my name," Hank said as he ducked around the corner to block the noise from the game. "How are things with you?"

Hannah looked over at her father passed out in his chair. "Just like old times." Then she started to get upset.

"Are you all right?" Hank asked. "What's happening?"

"I'm OK… I just *miss* you. This sucks."

"I miss you too."

"Do you have plans for tomorrow?" she asked as she rubbed her eyes.

"Just family stuff. Hopefully the championship will be over by then."

"How long does it last?"

"It's been known to drag on for two or three days."

"My God," she exclaimed. "That is so dorky."

"Thanks."

"Hank?"

"Yeah?"

"What are we doing?"

He sighed. "I don't know…"

Hannah looked out the window. It was snowing in Chicago. "Is it snowing where you are?"

"It is."

"Same here. When we get back to Grimwood, should we talk about things?"

"I'd like that," Hank said.

***

Christmas came and went, and the storms continued to pass through, each one bringing a fresh layer of powdery snow.

"I feel like we're living in the grandfather's memories from *A Child's Christmas in Wales*," Loren said one day as they were walking down to the beach after the most recent storm had blown out to sea. "Is it always like this?"

"Not really. There was a winter years and years ago that came close, but it was still nothing like this. This is amazing."

They walked alongside the seawall, the sand and snow crunching under their boots. Loren studied the pier. Enormous icicles had formed beneath the boardwalk, where they grew thicker with every crashing wave. They looked like rows of dinosaur teeth.

It had been a magical week; the days between Christmas and New Year's Eve drifting by in their own reality. Aside from one more visit from Olga, it had been just the two of them. At one point, Loren slipped away to call her parents and wish them Merry Christmas, but as far as she knew, the phone hadn't rung at the house. She didn't think Braden had spoken to his father at all. He certainly hadn't mentioned him.

Yet, while David McNutt never came up, Pops remained a frequent topic of discussion. His impact on Braden's life was clearly immeasurable. Loren wished she could have met him. Even now, his presence was evident everywhere Braden took her.

When they went sledding, As they walked by the water. On their trips to town. In the way they prepared meals. And especially in the things Braden did around the house to make sure everything was working properly, always there was the suggestion that these were the things Pops would have done.

"It's like living a lifetime in a week," Loren murmured as she watched the waves crash against the icy piers.

"What was that?" Braden asked as the wind tussled his hair.

Loren smiled. "Nothing, just a thought that popped into my head."

"Make sure you write it down," Braden said. Always thinking like a writer.

Loren shielded her eyes and smiled. She leaned in and kissed him.

"What was that for?"

"Just because"

~

They stayed up to watch the ball drop in Times Square.

The next morning, they packed their bags and loaded up the car.

It was Loren's birthday.

"I hate to leave," Loren said.

"We can come back any time," Braden reassured her.

"I hope so."

Loren waited at the car as Braden closed the house up. She didn't want to go back to Grimwood. Back to classes and the routine. She wanted to stay here for another week. Or forever. At least Braden would be with her.

Thank God they had finally worked things out.

When Braden walked back, he was carrying a small package in his hands. It was wrapped in brown paper. A book of course.

"Happy birthday," he said as he handed it over.

"You didn't have to get me another gift."

"Of course I did."

"Should I open it now?"

"Whenever you like. It's *your* gift."

Loren debated. "I'll open it when we get to Grimwood," she said as she tucked the package into her bag. "Something to look forward to."

Braden climbed into the driver's seat as she settled in beside him.

"Next stop, reality," he said as they started down the driveway.

Loren looked in the side view mirror, watching the big white house on Vineyard Avenue slip away behind her.

~

The drive back was long and tedious.

They stopped twice along the way. Once to get a bite to eat. Once to fill up on gas.

They talked.

They listened to music.

The weather and roads were clear.

It was all routine. Mundane. And fleeting.

Shortly before they reached Grimwood, two exits from the place where the two of them first met, Loren fell asleep. On the opposite side of the highway, a truck driver – a man they would never meet – did the same.

Later, Loren would learn the driver had been forced to work a double shift, and nodded off as he was returning home to see his family. He passed out at the wheel as he rounded a turn, jumped the median, and barreled into oncoming traffic.

She slept through it.

Braden glanced over at Loren and smiled. Then he heard the squealing of brakes and looked up to see the grill of a tractor-trailer barreling toward them.

They collided head on.

A gut-numbing explosion of metal and glass.

And Braden McNutt died on impact.

* * *

Sounds and images floated to the surface as Loren drifted in and out of consciousness. Rotor blades whirled overhead, churning up billowing clouds of snow. She was strapped to a gurney and loaded into a helicopter. The sudden, nauseating lurch of liftoff. Her eyes closed as the world dropped away.

7.

Loren awoke in Grimwood hospital.

She stared at the ceiling panels overhead as she attempted to get her bearings. She looked down, feeling a sharp pain at the base of her skull. There was a padded brace around her neck; it pinched the skin beneath her chin.

Her eyes scanned the room as hospital sounds clamored in the background. Calls and intercoms. Monitors whirring and pinging.

She was lying in a bed. She could feel bandages wrapped tightly around her body beneath the blue hospital sheets. Her left arm was in a brace.

Pain and numbness pulsed simultaneously throughout her body.

Her eyes shifted toward the soft glow of light seeping around the edges of the window curtains. Then she fell back to sleep.

~

Loren woke again with tears in her eyes.

She looked up to see Cathie Pepper standing over her, studying a chart.

"Hey there," Cathie said as she sat down beside her, gently taking Loren's right hand in her own. "I was hoping you might wake up on my shift."

Cathie brushed the hair from Loren's eyes and gave her a reassuring smile. Loren recognized the pinched look of sadness in her eyes. When Cathie squeezed her hand, Loren knew for certain…

Braden was gone.

~

The days faded in and faded out.

Whenever Loren came to, however briefly, Cathie would fill her in on what was happening, what procedures had been undertaken to save her life, and what was still to come.

There were emergency operations and transfusions.

Hannah and Hank donated blood.

"They're both O-negative," Cathie noted. "That was Jason's blood type as well."

The unvarnished facts as Cathie Pepper dispensed them were as follows. A truck driver headed in the opposite direction on the thruway had fallen asleep behind the wheel, crossed the barrier, and hit their car head on. Braden was killed instantly. The driver had escaped largely unscathed. And Loren suffered a variety of injuries. Whiplash. A badly broken arm. Broken ribs. And a collapsed lung.

Her friends were all there. They'd hurried to the hospital the moment they heard about the accident. When she felt up to it, Loren could see them. But she wasn't ready. Not yet.

Though her mind and body ached, the weight of what had happened was still sinking in. It didn't feel real. There must have been some mistake. And yet… tears seeped from her eyes. He heart knew the truth. When she again lost consciousness, the enveloping darkness was a relief.

~

"Loren?"

A familiar voice echoed in the void.

"Loren."

Her eyes opened slowly, and her father's smiling face was looking down at her.

"Dad."

"Your mother and I are here."

"What… day is it?"

"It's Wednesday."

"Where is Mom?"

"She just slipped downstairs to get some coffee."

Rick Austin was sitting in a chair beside his daughter's hospital bed, holding her hand. He looked older than the last time she'd seen him. Growing up, her friends always said her father looked like Robert Redford in *The Natural*, now he was edging closer to *Sneakers*-era Redford.

"When did you get here?" Loren asked.

"We've been here since the second operation."

"When was that?"

"Yesterday."

Loren tried to pull her father's face into focus. Her eyes settled on the pinched vertical line at the bridge of his nose.

"So you know about Braden?" she asked.

Rick nodded. "I'm so sorry. We've heard so many great things about him. Your mother loved him when she was here."

"I did too," Loren choked out.

He squeezed her hand. "Your friends have been wonderful getting us to and from the hospital."

Loren lay there, silent, as the tears streamed down her cheeks.

"This is a little late," her father said quietly. "But happy birthday, Loren."

Loren coughed a single, painful laugh in spite of herself. "Thanks."

She suddenly remembered the gift Braden had given her, and wondered what had become of it.

"You're up!" Mary Beth said as she entered the room and took Loren's free hand.

For the first time in years, Loren and her parents sat together, circling the wagons as they came to terms with the situation.

* * *

"To be honest," Loren said "I'm not sure what good you and Elissa are to me if I can't take your blood."

"We aren't a match!" Brooke protested.

"In our defense, we both donated for other patients while Hank and Hannah were getting juiced," Elissa added.

"That makes us sound like sketchy weightlifters," Hannah said.

"I appreciate it either way." Loren shifted her weight uncomfortably in the hospital bed. "So, the funeral is this weekend?"

Hank nodded. "We're heading down there tomorrow."

Loren's eyes glistened as she looked at their faces. "All of you?"

"Yeah," Brooke said quietly.

"I feel like I should be there."

"You need to recover," Hannah said.

"We'll be there for you," Brooke reassured her.

"Can you imagine how mad Braden would be with us if we let you travel right now?" Hank asked.

He squeezed Hannah's hand and Loren studied their interlaced fingers.

At least *something* was making sense again.

"How are you guys getting there?"

"The train," Brooke said.

"Good."

"I don't know about the rest of you," Hannah said to Brooke and Elissa as she and Hank headed for the door, "but we still need to get home and get packed."

Loren again noted their unacknowledged but apparent reconciliation.

"We better get going soon too," Elissa said.

"Can we get you anything?" Brooke asked Loren.

"I'm fine."

"I'll call you before we leave. And I'm sure Cathie will be on top of things."

"That's always a safe bet," Loren agreed.

Loren lay in silence after the group left. It was the first time in a long while that she'd been alone with her thoughts. Her eyes scanned the room. Before they headed back to their hotel for the night, her parents had brought over a few of Loren's things. Notebooks and pens. Textbooks and novels. Her father had set them in a neat stack on a table across from the bed. To the side of the books she noticed one item set off by itself. Somehow, it had made it through the accident unscathed, the brown paper neatly folded and taped in place as though the world around it was unchanged. Braden's birthday gift to her.

She couldn't get to it now, and she wasn't prepared to deal with it yet anyways. She welcomed the distraction of visits from her parents and her friends, but having the time to think was every bit as important to her. Like never before, Loren felt the need to find her own footing. Tearing that brown paper away would only knock her legs out from under her before she was ready.

* * *

It hadn't even been two years since Jason's death, yet here they were, once more saying goodbye to a friend. Hank unbuttoned his blazer to get some air as Hannah set her arm on his back.

"You all right?" she asked.

He nodded.

Brooke and Elissa glanced their way, then returned to the programs for the service.

There was a surprisingly large crowd in the church. Judging by the sea of grey hair, Hank suspected the majority of the people in attendance had been friends with Braden's grandfather.

His eyes fell on the black coffin at the foot of the altar.

A man with slicked back black hair was seated in the front row. As mourners filed in, many of them stopped to speak to him, or looked in his direction as they quietly took their seats.

That must be Braden's father.

A striking woman with silver hair, who looked to be in her early forties, came slowly down the aisle. She walked to the front of the church and stood for a moment, ten feet from the coffin, holding a hammered silver locket at her chest. She wore a variety of thin leather bracelets on each wrist, small turquois beads were woven into the bands, the color contrasted with her black dress. Hank's eye's narrowed curiously as she approached Braden's coffin, placed one hand on the glossy finish, and bowed her head. She looked up after a time, gave Braden's father a solemn nod, and receded to the back of the church.

~

They were gathered in front of the church after the service, discussing how best to get to the reception, when a blond girl with red eyes began to walk past them.

"Kate?" Brooke asked.

Kate looked up, caught by surprise.

"Brooke?" Then she recognized Hank and Hannah. "I didn't know you were all here."

They exchanged hugs.

"That was a nice service," Kate said.

"It was," Hank agreed.

"How is Loren doing?"

"She's recovering," Hannah said. "But it's going to be a long haul."

"Yeah." Kate wiped at her eyes. "Please send her my best."

"Are you going to the reception?" Brooke asked.

"I don't think so," she said, shaking her head. "I need to get headed back to Grimwood tonight."

"When did you get here?"

"Yesterday. You?"

"This morning," Hank said.

"Well, it was good seeing you all," Kate stammered as she excused herself. "Well, not good, but I'm glad we crossed paths."

"Who was that?" Elissa asked Brooke after Kate had left.

"That was Braden's girlfriend freshman year."

"*Really?* Why have I never heard about her?" Elissa asked.

"He was too hung up on Loren," Brooke said. "But she must have really cared about him."

~

The reception was held in a ballroom overlooking the eighteenth hole at the Huntington Country Club. There was no music, just the quiet din of conversation and the sounds of waiters clearing away empty dishes.

Brooke picked at a plate of food and watched from a distance as Hank and Hannah walked over and introduced themselves to

Braden's father. It was a brief conversation. A few words back and forth, a quick handshake, then he turned back to the person he'd been talking to, and Hank and Hannah were on their way.

A silver-haired woman in a formfitting black dress stood a short distance away, sipping on a glass of ginger ale and looking out the window. Her right hand kept returning to a locket at her chest. She glanced over at Brooke.

"Hi," Brooke said.

"Hello."

"Were you at the service?"

"I was." The woman walked closer. "You?"

Brooke nodded.

"I'm Brooke by the way."

"Linda."

"How did you know Braden?"

Linda cleared her throat. "He was my son."

"Oh, I had no idea," Brooke exclaimed. "I'm so sorry."

"Thank you. Although, I don't feel as if I should even be here."

"Why?"

"It's complicated. To be honest, I was never really a part of his life." She motioned with her glass toward Braden's father. "I don't know that either of us had any business having a child. Thank goodness for David's parents."

"Braden talked about Pops a lot."

"Pops." Linda smiled. "Are you one of Braden's friends from school?"

"I am. There are four of us here."

"Do you know anything about the girl who was in the car with him?"

"Loren. She's my roommate actually."

"Oh. How is she doing?"

"About as well as can be expected I suppose."

Brooke went over everything Loren had gone through since the accident.

"Physically, she's recovering. Emotionally, she's where we all are. I mean, you know…"

Linda again held the locket at her heart as her head bobbed knowingly. After a moment of hesitation, she took the piece of jewelry from around her neck and place it in Brooke's hand.

"Can you give this to your friend?"

Brooke looked down as Linda pressed the latch release with her nail. The locket's cover flipped open to reveal a black and white picture of a smiling baby.

Braden.

"Are you sure you want to give this away?" Brooke asked.

"I'm positive. I have other pictures of him. But if your friend and Braden-" She paused to regain her composure. "If they were that much in love, Loren deserves to have that picture more than I ever did."

"I doubt that's true," Brooke said as she studied Braden's twinkling eyes in the photo. "But I know she'll be honored to have it."

* * *

"It's strange to think Braden had a mother that even he didn't know." Loren studied the image inside the locket. "It looks like him though, same glint in the eyes."

"I thought the same thing," Brooke said. "She seemed kind. Very pretty, but quiet. She certainly appeared to have her act together, but maybe that came with time. Did Braden ever tell you anything about her?"

"Not really. I don't think he knew much about her. Or maybe he did, but he kept it to himself. As well as I knew Braden, there's lot about him I suspect will always be a mystery"

"Speaking of mysteries, has Hank had any luck finding Braden's laptop or book?"

Loren shook her head. "He checked Braden's apartment when you all got back, but he couldn't find anything anywhere. I hope nothing has happened to it."

"Could he have left it at the house, or in the car?"

"He didn't bring it with him."

"It will turn up," Brooke said.

"I hope so."

"How are you doing with your physical therapy?"

"I won't be winning any races anytime soon, but I'm making headway. My folks say I'm improving."

"And how do you think *they're* doing?"

"Better than I would have expected. I guess it helps to get them working on something together again," Loren said. "If I'd known this was what it would take to get them talking, I'd have gotten into a deadly car accident years ago."

Brooke seemed taken aback by the comment.

"Sorry," Loren said. "Gallows humor."

~

Recovery was slow.

It's just me and my demons, Loren thought to herself as she waited for the physical therapist and her parents to arrive.

She was seated on the edge of her bed, dressed in grey sweatpants and a matching top. A very "Garp-ian outfit" as Braden would have put it. She stared down at her bare feet. Her lower extremities had escaped the accident unscathed, but the rest of her injuries, and the invasiveness of the subsequent surgeries, had left her in rough shape.

She was working with a physical therapist to regain her

strength. Her sessions with Christy involved lots of stretching, some work with weights, and long walks through the hospital corridors.

The walks were a good reminder of all that went on in the hospital. Much more than met the human eye. Babies were born here. Patients came for life-saving procedures. And people died.

Jason Pepper had died here.

That was still hard to believe. How many others had slipped away here over the years? More than Loren could possibly comprehend. What happened to them? Did any of them stay behind? Did they flare?

Most likely.

What about Braden?

Unlike Jason, Braden hadn't made it to the hospital. He was gone in a blink, in the middle of a snowy highway. What had become of him? Did he pass to the other side, or was he still around somewhere? Could flares drift from one place to another, or were they relegated to the location of their passing? Surely they went to the places that meant the most to them, locations that harbored some unresolved element of their living lives.

Christy and her parents emerged in the corridor outside Loren's room. She could hear her mother grilling the physical therapist on the specifics of their workouts. Finally, the murmurs died down, and Christy leaned in through the doorway.

"Is it a Swiffer day or a non-Swiffer day?" she asked.

Swiffers were Christy's name for the nonwoven fabric booties the hospital gave patients in lieu of slippers. Her theory was that they were really a ploy to trim the janitorial budget by having the patients unwittingly dry mop the corridors themselves.

"What's the temperature?" Loren asked.

"Outside? It's right between skull splitting and finger snapping."

"Then I guess it's a Swiffer day," Loren said as she pulled the itchy coverings onto her feet.

* * *

"How do my parents seem to you?" Loren asked Christy as they made their way around the hospital corridors. Christy had her carrying a five pound dumbbell in her right arm.

"Your parents? They seem concerned, but upbeat."

"Do they seem happy?"

Christy studied her patient's face. "I take it we're talking about factors outside of your treatment?"

"Yeah."

"They don't seem all that different from a lot of the parents I see from day to day."

"Is that good or bad?"

"I guess… neither?"

"Do you meet a lot of couples who live largely separate lives?"

"Probably. But it's not my place to judge. No one knows the ins and outs of someone else's relationship. Even the people *in* the relationships seldom understand what's going on."

Loren walked slowly, rubbing her right hand under her ribcage.

"I've always expected my parent's to get divorced one day. It seems inevitable."

"Why's that?"

"They just don't seem to be… in love to me. I don't know that they ever have."

"They seem to get along fine to me," Christy said. "Between the two of them, they certainly know the ins and outs of your treatment and what's happening from day to day."

"That's probably because they've run a business together for decades. They're good with their Ps and Qs, it's just…"

"The vowels that trip them up? Maybe they're Bill and Hillary types. They have their common interests and their individual worlds. There are certainly worse things in life."

"Maybe you're right," Loren said.

But she couldn't help but think there were far *better* options as well.

"So, on a different topic, if I'm only doing the one weight, am I eventually going to come out of this cast with a scrawny, hairy left arm, and a totally jacked right? I don't totally get the goal here."

"There is no goal," Christy deadpanned. "I just thought it would look cool. If you want, I can get you some purple ankle weights like those speed-walking grannies wear. It might help you buff the floors a little better while you're at it."

Loren laughed in spite of herself. "I'm good for now. But thanks."

~

Later that night, when her father had gone with Hank to check out the Grimwood Brewery, Loren took advantage of the time alone with her mother to feel out how things were going. Mary Beth was flying home the next morning, so if Loren was going to broach the subject, this was the time to do it.

"So you're heading back tomorrow?"

"I am, unless you need me to stay. I can always change my ticket."

Loren shook her head. "You've already done plenty. Dad will still be here."

"I had to push him to go out tonight," her mother said. "He's worried about you."

"He doesn't need to worry. I'm fine."

"You are not fine, Loren. You've been through a lot. You've had a horrible loss. Don't feel like you need to rush through your recovery to make any of us feel better."

"OK," Loren murmured.

She couldn't think of anything more to say.

She certainly wasn't all right, but what was she supposed to do, sob uncontrollably? Punch holes in her hospital room's walls? There was nothing she could do to stop what she was feeling, to dull the all-consuming ache in her chest. If she had ever doubted the idea that people die of broken hearts, she sure as hell believed it now. Her heart *hurt*. It had nothing to do with her injuries, or any of her surgeries. She'd finally opened herself up to something she had sensed and feared since the first day she met Braden, and now that he was gone, nothing remained but an overwhelming, smothering sense of loss.

Yet that was something she couldn't discuss with Mary Beth Austin. Her family didn't address such emotions in so many words. They tiptoed around them by discussing other matters, like business and beer. Puzzlebox Brewery, more than anything else, save *perhaps* for their children, was the bond that held Loren's parents together.

"Whatever happened with that company that wanted to buy the brewery?" Loren asked out of the blue.

"Poptop Distributing? It's nearly a done deal."

"I wasn't sure if it was still happening."

"Yes, very much so. They're just waiting for us to sign. They sent over the final paperwork just before… Right around the end of the year. Our lawyer has been looking it over to be sure it includes everything we agreed to. As soon as we're both back in Durango, we should close the deal."

"Oh, so that's it then."

As far as Loren was concerned, her parents signing off on the sale of their business was tantamount to signing their divorce papers. As far as their relationship was concerned, the brewery and their marriage were one and the same.

"What are you guys going to do next?"

"Probably what we've been discussing. I'll stay with Puzzlebox and your father will have some time to explore his options."

Loren fell silent. He'd been 'exploring his options' for years now.

"Is something the matter?" her mother asked finally.

"Why don't you guys just get a divorce?"

"I don't ~ Where is this coming from?"

"Do you even *want* to be married anymore, Mom?"

"I guess I-" She stopped to gather her thoughts. "I guess I don't."

"Would you just do me a favor? Actually, would you do Dad a favor? Once you guys sell the brewery, could you just get a divorce so the two of you can move on?"

Her mother opened her mouth to speak. He face flushed as if she was ready to get angry, but she held back, and slowly, the color drained from her face.

"There will be plenty of time to talk about that later. I'll be leaving tomorrow. Your father will be in town for another few days to help you get settled at your apartment. If there's anything you need to help you recuperate or get back into the swing of things at the University, be sure you tell us, OK?"

Loren was still in Limbo. Only now she felt the added guilt of having broached a topic that was none of her business. Though… she suspected Braden would have argued that it was. Either way, what was the point?

What was the point of anything now? Getting out of the hospital was the ostensible "goal" of her recovery. Regaining the strength to resume her classes was the unstated purpose of her work with Christy. But moving on with her *life*, that was something Loren couldn't yet imagine.

She and her mother said their goodbyes. There was no more talk of business deals or divorces.

Loren sat on her bed and studied the table at the far end of her room. Her eyes once more fell on the birthday gift from Braden.

It felt like years had passed since that day.

Loren stared at the brown wrapping paper. She still didn't feel ready, but now was as good a time as any. She set her bare feet on the cold linoleum floor, shifted her weight out of bed, and slowly made her way to the table, where she picked up the gift – its weight felt strangely familiar in her hands – and carefully tore away the paper, until she was staring at the cover of *The Wizard of Oz*. Braden had wrapped up the original copy she'd admired in his grandfather's library. Somehow, as she sat on this side of the new reality, it seemed like the perfect, whimsical conclusion to a week of tragedy.

8.

Among the get well wishes waiting for her at the apartment was a card signed by everyone at the bookstore. That was another place Loren would again have to face. Another stop along the journey of "firsts." Neither Elissa nor Brooke were home. Though Loren was thankful for the quiet, a little distraction might have helped. Returning to her apartment felt like another strange detour. After basically moving in with Braden, then having Hannah practically assume her place, moving back felt like a return to her not so distant but far removed past.

Her father carried her bags in behind her and set them in her room. He walked back into the living room and found her staring down at the card from her coworkers.

"Do you want to get out of here?" he asked.

"Yeah, I think I would."

~

Just as Loren suspected, The Dinosaur Bar-B-Que was right up her father's alley. In an alternate timeline, The Dinosaur was *exactly* the kind of place Rick Austin might have started himself.

Loren eased into her seat, resting her left arm on the table to get some relief from the weight of her cast as she looked around the room. Then she downed her first beer, setting the glass down with a *thunk*.

Her father did a double take when he turned back from the stage and saw Loren's empty glass. Not one to judge someone for drowning their sorrows, he didn't say anything when the waitress came by with their food and Loren ordered another round.

Their drinks came and Loren made short work of her second beer as well. Rick once again took notice. He'd seen his daughter drink before. He owned a brewery after all, it was inevitable that his kids would partake in the family product, but he was also well attuned to warning signs. The next time the waitress came by, he asked for the bill.

They walked back to Loren's apartment. Brooke and Elissa had returned while they were out. Loren was loose from her drinks, but not overtly intoxicated. It wasn't until she stumbled on the edge of the carpet that her roommates realized she'd been drinking and stepped in to help.

"Did you guys have a good night?" Brooke asked as she encouraged Loren to take a seat on the couch.

Loren didn't answer.

"We went back to The Dinosaur," Rick said. "It continues to live up to its reputation."

"Yeah, that's always a good time," Elissa said.

"I've got to go back to my classes," Loren mumbled out of nowhere.

"Not for a couple more days though, right?" Brooke asked.

"Day after tomorrow," Rick interjected. "And only if she's up for it."

Brooke turned to Loren. "You'll be ready, right?"

Loren remained quiet.

"She's keeping her options open," Elissa joked.

Rick wasn't sure *what* was happening.

Loren leaned her head against the couch cushion and closed her eyes

"You tired?" Rick asked.

"You should go to bed, Loren. Catch up on some sleep," Brooke said. Then to Rick, "Why don't you head back to your hotel, we'll look after her."

"Are you sure?"

Brooke nodded. "We'll hang out a little bit, then call it a night."

After a moment's hesitation, Rick kissed Loren on the forehead, excused himself, and slipped out the front door.

* * *

Winston Churchill called his melancholy "The Black Dog" – a creature forever snapping at his heels, or lying across his path, unwilling to move aside. For others, depression isn't so much an entity, as a filter that colors everything they see and experience, highlighting only the cruelest sides of reality.

For Loren, depression seeped in slowly, pooling around her in silence, until the force of the current swept her downstream. By the time she realized what was happening, it had pulled her out to sea.

After her father flew home, she somehow managed to return to her previous schedule. Not to her life; but to the timetable of the places she was expected to be, the things she was expected to do.

Classes were alien to her. She sat in the lectures and listened to the lessons, but she took nothing in.

She had the same sensation at the bookstore. Shifts went by, and she couldn't recall what she'd done. She waited on customers. She searched for books. She stood at the front counter and replayed mental recordings of conversations gone by. Her body was in one place, but her mind was always somewhere else.

When she was with Cole, there were times she would take a mental step back and observe the way she was going about her life – making decisions and weighing her options – and at her most lucid, she suspected there was an aspect of woeful indifference that kept her involved with a guy she didn't entirely care for. But this was something different. What she was working through was a sort of oozing misery she couldn't entirely comprehend. It seeped into her body and settled in her joints. It flooded her thoughts and overwhelmed her emotions. Nothing she felt or said seemed to come from inside. They were echoes, transmissions from another life.

Her grades slipped.

She didn't write.

She didn't read.

She slept.

She drank too much. One beer became three. Three beers became five.

Her head throbbed in the mornings. In the afternoons between classes, she slept in the armchairs in the lobby of the Student Union.

At work, she began taking Karl up on the offer to join him for a cigarette, and soon, for the first time since high school, she was smoking regularly. She tucked a crumpled pack in her bag, and always kept extras tucked away in her room. When she wasn't smoking, she would sit in lectures, smelling the nicotine on her fingertips and waiting for the end of session so she could slip out into the wet cold and light up.

She walked curious routes around campus, steering clear of the library. She never ate at Brownie's. When she couldn't avoid The Writing Center altogether, she would keep her distance from certain seats and corridors.

She was avoiding Braden.

That much she knew.

Not Braden himself. Not a flare or his memory. She was avoiding the spots he used to go. The places *they* used to go. It wasn't that she was trying to forget him. That was impossible. The truth was that he was *always* on her mind. A joke would come to her, or a turn of phrase, and she'd think, "I can't wait to tell that to Braden." Then she would remember…

She could have told her friends. Brooke would have jumped at the chance to help, but Loren wasn't talking. Not at the moment. Mentally, she'd gone underground to weather the fallout of her loss. What exactly that would entail, and what awaited her on the other side, she did not know.

Finally, around the end of Winter quarter, the realization struck her that unless she stepped up her studies and locked in, she wasn't going to graduate on time. Mentally, she wasn't ready, but physically, she had every intention of powering through. The cast came off. Her pain was subsiding. Physically, she was beginning to recover, but she'd lost quite a bit of ground academically. That meant she would have to stick around Grimwood for the summer session.

9.

AT THE START OF Spring quarter, Loren finally got up the nerve to walk past the library. She'd given Braden's old stomping ground a wide berth since the accident, so just walking by and casting a wary eye up at the tower felt like a victory.

She didn't go in. Not yet. That was a challenge for another day.

"We need to have a party," Elissa proclaimed as they ate dinner at Red Tomato that night.

"Why?" Brooke asked.

"Why?" Elissa countered. "Why *not?* I'm finished with my co-op. Hannah is finished with *her* co-op-"

"Hallelujah," Hannah interjected.

"-It's spring," Elissa continued. "Training is starting back up for the team. And we have *yet* to throw a party at our apartment. I think it's high time we shake the dust off and have some fun."

The table looked at Loren uncertainly.

"It sounds good to me," she said. "I could use a little fun."

* * *

Saturday night, the girls' apartment was filled with crew team members, their significant others, and friends of friends. Elissa slid back into the team ranks as if she'd never been away.

Now that her relationship with Elissa was public knowledge, Brooke was able to enjoy herself at this party as well, sipping Diet Cokes while Elissa hoisted cans of Genesee.

Sometime after midnight, Hank joined Loren for a cigarette on the front steps.

He inhaled deeply and choked on the smoke, coughing furiously until he caught his breath. "Now I remember why I gave these up," he wheezed as he scraped the butt out on the bottom of his shoe and took a seat on the stairs.

"Yeah," Loren said as she rocked back on her feet and took a long drag. Her face lit up in the warm glow of hot ash. "I need to do the same, but I can't seem to find the willpower."

Hank studied her expression, but kept his mouth shut.

"How are you and Hannah doing?" Loren asked.

"Surprisingly well, actually. It feels like we're back to normal."

"I'm glad to hear it."

Hank took a swig of Genesee. The beer sloshed in the bottle as he leaned forward. "How are you?"

"Eh, you know."

"You *seem* a little better," he observed.

"Do I? I feel less... raw. But... I don't really know what I'm going to do."

"Can I let you in on a little secret?" he asked.

"What's that?"

"None of us do."

Loren sucked air though her teeth. They were beginning to tingle. Though she'd lost count of her drinks that night, she'd clearly had more than enough.

"So, I've been putting this off for a while," Hank began. "But there's something I need to bring up... I got a call from Braden's father this week."

Loren's eyes narrowed.

"He's wondering if we might be able to clear Braden's apartment out for him."

"He wants *us* to do that? Doesn't he want to see where his son was living?"

"I know," Hank said gently. "I thought the same thing, but he thinks it should be us. Or you."

"Why me?!" Loren exclaimed.

"Apparently there's some sort of letter. You should have gotten a notice from a law firm."

"A law firm?" Loren looked confused. "I haven't gotten any letter. What's it about?"

"Well…" Hank began tentatively "It seems Braden made you the beneficiary of his estate. I don't know what that entails exactly, but according to his father, you get everything."

"Oh." Loren drew one hand to her to chest, touching the locket tucked beneath her shirt. "For real?"

"Apparently, so."

"Why would he – *Could* he even do that?"

"It sounds like Braden could and he *did*," Hank said. "And come on, we both know why."

Loren paused to collect her thoughts. "I don't think I should accept it."

"I really think you should," Hank said. "It's what he wanted."

"And his father, he's not stopping it somehow?"

"Either he's not or he *can't*, but it sounds like he's just following Braden's instructions."

"That's… overwhelming," Loren said as she blinked back tears.

Hank waited for the news to set in before he spoke again.

"Did you have any thoughts on when you might want to go over there?"

"Maybe this weekend?" Loren asked.

Hank nodded. "Sounds good."

* * *

The cracked bar of soap brought Loren back to reality.

She'd just walked into the apartment and taken a quick look around when her eyes began to well up.

"I'll give you a minute," Hank said as he stepped back into the hall.

Loren slipped into the bathroom to splash cold water on her face. As she watched the water swirling down the drain, she glanced over at the bar of soap sitting on the edge of the sink, where either she or Braden had set it before Christmas. The soap had dried and split down the middle over the course of the ensuing months.

Braden's apartment was untouched. There were happy, intimate memories here. Nights and weekends together in that small space. The kitchen was scrubbed clean, but dusty. The bed was just as they'd left it. Unmade. The comforter thrown back, pillows still dented from the weight of their heads.

Yet, even as the space *looked* the same, it now felt hollow. There'd always been a Spartan quality to the place, but without Braden, it seemed empty.

Loren walked to the desk and gathered up her notebooks. She stacked her things on the corner of the kitchen counter, along with Braden's books and a few other keepsakes. Then she resumed the search for his writing. She opened the closets and cabinets, scouring them for Braden's computer, notebooks, and manuscripts.

Hank wrapped gently on the doorframe. "Is it OK if I come in?"

Loren nodded.

"Still no sign of it?" he asked.

"Nothing."

Hank joined the search, but several hours later, after turning the place upside down, they were still coming up empty-handed.

"Wherever his writing is, it's not here," Hank concluded.

Where could he have put everything? Loren wondered.

Hank took in the ransacked room. "You're *sure* he didn't take it home with him?"

"I *know* he didn't."

She was baffled.

The incident with Harper and the kitchen fire down the hall had spooked him. Braden must have taken all his work out of the apartment. Maybe someone at the store had an idea where it was. She'd have to ask around.

"Just let me know what you want me to bring over to your place," Hank said. "I'll get some boxes later and start packing things up."

"That would be great," Loren said as her gaze settled on Braden's collection of Alan Grimwood titles. "I'll just take a few things with me now."

After Loren left, Hank – with the help of some of the guys from the Red Tomato – spent the remainder of the weekend clearing everything out.

Loren never again set foot in Braden's apartment.

* * *

Loren sat at her desk, reading for one of her classes and absent-mindedly rubbing her side. She slipped her fingers under her shirt and ran her fingertips over the scars along her ribcage, feeling the raised lines where the doctors had sutured the incisions. Then she leaned back, her eyes falling on the line-up of Alan Grimwood titles above her desk. She'd shelved Braden's copies alongside her own. She took down the hardbound editions Braden had given her as gifts over the years and looked through them, flipping to the front to read his inscriptions, each scrawled in Braden's signature blend of looping cursive and slashing chicken scratch. He'd always ended his notes with "love, Braden" – even before it was probably appropriate to do so. Never really hiding how he felt.

It was the first comfortably warm night of the season, a hint of things to come. Her bedroom window was open and she could hear buses rumbling up The Ave one block over. She grabbed a sweatshirt and walked out into the living room.

Brooke and Elissa were stretched out on the couch, watching a movie.

Brooke looked over her shoulder as Loren stepped out of her room. "Where are you headed?"

"Just going for a walk."

"Do you want company?" Elissa asked.

"No thanks, I'm fine."

~

Apparently no one was in the mood to stay inside studying. The Avenue was bustling with students. The light was dimming, but the sky was touched with pink as Loren walked down 75th and crossed the street at the base of the old stairs. She cut across the sports fields behind the residential side, with no destination in mind, just an instinctive need to drift through campus.

The track team was training as she crossed the back field. By the time she reached the woods behind Brownie's, the sun had dipped below the trees. The fading light cast halos around the green buds on the branches overhead. The residential side was oddly quiet, almost as if she had the campus to herself. She peered around the woods as she walked, recalling the first time she'd observed a flare weaving in and out amongst the trees.

Grimwood.

Thinking of it now, she wondered why she hadn't been scared. Why even the most startling encounters had never left her frightened, but mostly just… chilled. There was a sadness in each of the instances in which she'd encountered flares. As if their appearance was tied to the emotions of those who crossed paths with them. She half expected to see one tonight, but who would she have to tell about it now that Braden was gone. Loren's stomach tensed, a fleeting ache of loneliness.

She walked along the side of Brownie's and out onto the quad. There was the statue. The scene of that long ago moment that had caused so much heartache.

She walked the quarter mile to the academic side, where she drifted among the silent buildings, past The Writing Center, past The Lookout, and stopping, finally, in front of Grimwood Library.

Had this been her destination all along?

Loren climbed the steps and stood at the entrance, gathering her thoughts. Summoning the courage to go inside. She gripped the handle on one of the massive double doors. Melancholy gave way to trepidation as she considered what exactly she was hoping to find inside. Was she hoping for closure? Did she just need to sink into the sadness and let it carry her to the next stage of mourning?

She didn't know, but she opened the door and walked inside.

Grimwood Library was the same as ever: Magnificent, haunting, intimidating, and utterly inspiring. To those who revered the written word – the power of ideas – *this* was the heart of the library. Braden had likened it to something from a Jules Verne novel. The first floor, which was actually four stories high, contained thirty wide-planked study tables that stretched from one end of the room to the other. Iron catwalks and spiral staircases towered overhead, with three and four story bookcases, walkways, bridges, and balconies welded together in the upper reaches, an intricate skeleton of black metal wrapped around a temple of seemingly limitless knowledge. Everywhere, there were books. And above it all loomed an enormous, domed ceiling, painted with an eerily-realistic depiction of the night sky.

Loren strolled the aisles, studying the faces of the students scattered among the tables. Her eyes scanned each of the rows as she passed by. Her pulse racing. But she saw nothing unusual.

She climbed the stone steps in the library's farthest corner until she reached the top floor, emerging in an empty corridor. It was here that she and Braden had both experienced their most unsettling run-ins with flares. Loren hurried down the hall, unafraid, but on guard as she approached Ashton Study Hall.

She stepped into the wood-paneled room. It was exactly as she remembered it. How many hours and days had Braden spent holed up in this space, studying and writing? Other than the bookstore and perhaps the apartment, there was no place in Grimwood where he'd spent more time. It was the perfect space to get away from everything. Free of noise and distractions. Just Braden and his work.

And now, Braden McNutt was nowhere to be found.

His missing laptop and manuscripts weren't there either.

Like their owner, they seemed to have vanished into the ether.

Foolish as she felt, Loren scoured the room, searching through each of the workspaces, but in the end, she left the building emptyhanded.

Whatever Braden might have left behind, Loren had yet to find it.

***

Braden should have been in this class with her. The third course in the four-section spine of the Writing Center's primary curriculum.

Now it was just Loren.

Mark Price was once again the instructor, which seemed like an appropriate bookend.

Price's lectures were always interesting, which made Loren all the more frustrated when her mind began to wander. She kept thinking about the things she would have to do if she hoped to stay on track to graduate next year. Her recovery had occupied much of the past quarter, but staying for the summer would give her a chance to catch up.

Fortunately, she wouldn't have to change her living arrangements since Brooke and Elissa were also staying in town for the break. She could take her classes. Work at the store. And keep her head down until she was on track again.

Price was discussing writing and outlines.

"If you don't know where you're going in your work," he said. "How can you possibly expect to get there, or take your readers on a journey that is worth the trouble?"

The subject was prescient. But day to day life was complicated. The more you dwelled on your goal, the farther from your grasp it seemed to slip.

For a writer, it was equally important to know what kind of stories you wanted to tell. Braden had long ago told her he didn't 'want to write about sinister things,' a statement that had prompted much discussion of what that meant exactly.

Braden had a philosophy about storytelling, a style and set of ideals he wanted to instill in his work. She'd read his writing, and while he aimed for an escapist quality, Loren felt he touched upon more of life's unpleasant realities than he was willing to admit. He simply hid the darker elements under a sheen of excitement.

Dead Men Don't – their aborted project from freshman year – had possessed a *distinctly* macabre quality, much of it coming from Loren's approach to the story. Braden had added the flourishes of fun, while she'd brushed on layers of arsenic and gore.

"Is that the kind of thing *you* want to say?" he'd asked her.

She was beginning to think that maybe it was.

Either way, she was attending one of the best writing programs in the country. She'd kept her course load light for the final quarter, afraid she would be easily overwhelmed, but her mind was growing restless, anxious for something to chew on. It was time to get busy and figure things out!

She missed Braden, She *longed* for him. But he was gone.

She had to come to terms with that somehow. Perhaps words, writing and ideas, would help her find another way forward.

~

The store was quiet. It was one of those warm, spring nights, when the doors were open to let in a breeze, along with the occasional customer in search of something new. Loren waited on a handful of customers, but overall, she had the main sales floor to herself as she shelved books in the mystery section.

Janet Rylander had a new book out.

Now *that* was someone who liked to write about sinister things.

Loren brought the book over to the counter and was flipping through it when Karl walked by.

"You read her stuff?" he asked.

"I do."

"Pretty violent."

"I suppose, but it works."

Karl took a pack of cigarettes from his shirt pocket and motioned toward the back door. "I'm taking a break if you want to join me."

"What about the counter?"

"We can see it through the back window."

"All right."

The best part of smoking was that delicious smell when the tobacco fired up. It was all downhill from there, but that first, smoldering drag was almost worth it.

She handed Karl's lighter back to him as her eyes briefly settled on the darkened back window of Braden's apartment. She dreaded the day someone new moved in.

"How are you doing?" Karl asked.

"I'm OK."

"I'm working on scheduling for the summer. Do you have a sense of your plans yet?"

"I'll be in town," Loren replied.

"Are you interested in working some hours?"

"If you have them, I'll take everything I can get."

"Consider them gotten."

They were quiet for a moment as they enjoyed their smokes and took in the nighttime atmosphere.

"So, you like Janet Rylander?" Karl asked eventually.

"I do. I didn't realize she had something new out. I've been out of the loop."

"She's pretty good. Kind of a meat and potatoes writer."

Loren laughed. "A what?"

"You know, one of those dependable authors." He exhaled a cloud of smoke. "No literary bullshit, just solid, satisfying writing."

"I sometimes think that's the best kind."

"I agree."

"What do you like to read?" Loren asked.

"Me? I like Patrick McCabe."

"Who's that?"

He wrote *The Butcher Boy* and *The Dead School*."

"And you think *Janet Rylander* is dark?!"

Karl smiled. "It's different though, it's like a clean, organic darkness."

"I don't know." She gave him a skeptical smile. "Sounds like literary bullshit to me."

"Yeah." Karl laughed. "A little bit."

Loren finished her cigarette, mashed out the butt, and tossed it in the coffee can by the back door.

"It was nice talking books with you," she said as she looked inside and saw a customer waiting at the counter.

"You too," Karl said. "And I'll be sure to put you on the summer schedule."

~

Hannah set down her menu. "So, are you going to take it?"

"I think I should," Hank replied.

"I didn't even know you were looking at co-ops," she said. "When did you apply for this?"

"When we were on our break. I just sort of applied on a whim, and forgot about it until I got the letter today."

"And this record label is in New York?"

"Yeah. I'd be there for two months this summer. What do you think?"

"I mean, things are just getting back to normal again, but it sounds like you want to do it."

"It could help me get some really good experience," Hank said. "And you said you want to sort of reboot your major this summer anyway, so you'll be busy."

"You think we're doing well enough for a summer apart? A few months ago you weren't so sure."

"Well, I don't know why, but now I do." He reached across the table and took her hand. "I think we'll be just fine."

~

The letter arrived during the last week of classes. The return address showed it was from New York, so Loren initially thought it was for Brooke and left it with her mail.

"Hey," Brooke said that night as she knocked on the door of Loren's room and set the manila envelope on her desk. "This isn't mine."

"It's not?"

Loren picked it up and slid her nail under the flap, tearing it back to reveal a thick bundle of paper. She read through the pages, scanning the rows of numbers and figures.

Her mouth fell open.

"What is it?" Brooke asked.

Loren flipped through the rest of the document, then handed her the pages.

Brooke gave her a confused look and began reading.

Loren watched her roommate's expression when she reached the end of the document. Their eyes met.

"Holy shit."

Loren sighed. "I feel so guilty."

"What do you have to feel guilty about?"

"I have this immense sense of relief, like there's one less thing to worry about."

"And what's wrong with that?"

"Just the fact that he's gone. And I'm here, benefitting from it…"

"Loren, you can't think about it like that. Braden could never have known things would happen the way they did, but he obviously wanted to do whatever he could for you."

Loren still seemed uncertain.

"Look at it this way," Brooke continued. "Don't you think Braden would be happy to know this was making such a difference? I mean, think about what this means for you."

Loren nodded her head slowly.

It meant she would be free to find her own, without answering to anybody.

10.

THOUGH SHE'D NEVER ADMIT it, Betty had warmed to the group over the years. Perhaps not obviously, but as much as an older woman waiting tables at a college town greasy spoon like Brick's ever could. She would always, *always* take their orders in her signature no-nonsense, "don't waste my time" style, but she tended to do it with a subtle half-smile on her face after the first year. It was this way with thousands of students that had drifted through Grimwood over the past forty years. She seldom knew their names, but she knew their faces, was fleetingly aware of their relationships, and took note of how they changed over the course of their time at Grimwood.

It was the same with this bunch. She noticed who came in together. Who ate alone. And what went on when the entire contingent arrived for a meal and took their seats in their regular booth. One of the boys had passed away a couple years ago. He'd been a local. That was when she started bringing their drinks before they ordered. She didn't know if they noticed, she didn't give a damn, it was just something she started to do. When the boy's girlfriend started coming in with someone new, and that girl became a part of the group, Betty didn't say anything, but she occasionally forgot to charge them for dessert.

Around the start of the new year, the papers ran a story about a young man who'd been killed in a car accident on his way back from holiday break. The picture at the top of the page looked familiar. When Loren came in with her father, and Betty saw the condition she was in, she put the pieces together and realized what had happened. Twice in the course of three years, those kids had been sucker punched by tragedy. That was when she started forgetting to add drinks and extras to their tab. Again, whether they noticed or not, she didn't care, it was her way of paying tribute, helping out in what little way she could.

When they walked in the door tonight, it was clearly for an unofficial, end-of-year celebration. Betty prepped a tray of their preferred drinks, put in an order for five brick plates (it was undoubtedly that kind of night), and walked to their booth, where she dispensed their glasses with a half-smile and pretended to take their orders.

"I feel like we always have plates for the last meal of the year," Hank mused after Betty headed back to the kitchen.

"Probably because you always corner us into getting them," Hannah noted.

Loren looked around the table. "So, you're all leaving me tomorrow."

"No one is leaving for long," Hank said. "Well, other than me."

"How long will the rest of you be gone?"

"Elissa and I will only be away for a week," Brooke said.

"That's probably how long I'll stay in the city with Hank," Hannah noted. "I'll help him get settled in, maybe poke around for a couple days, then take the train back here and get to work."

"What are you gonna do with all that time?" Elissa asked Loren.

"That's a good question. Work at the bookstore. Read. Just kind of figure out what's next. Then the summer session starts up…"

"And I'll be right there with you," Hannah said. "Operation reboot."

"I'm sorry you're changing your major," Loren said. "But I'm relieved I won't be the only one taking summer classes."

"Glad I can help," Hannah deadpanned.

"And your co-op sounds awesome," Loren said to Hank.

"Making the dream a reality," Hannah mused.

"Jason would be proud," Brooke added.

The table grew quiet.

Loren was the first to break the silence. "And next year we're all seniors, can you believe it?"

Betty watched from the counter as the five friends raised their glasses, then the kitchen bell rang and she picked up their order.

"Boy, you guys are getting faster and faster," Hank said when she arrived at their table and started handing out their plates.

11.

LOREN HAD SELDOM FELT truly alone in her life. With two siblings, and a mother and father who sought out crowds in order to avoid the long stretches of silence at home, it seemed there was *always* a whirl of activity around her.

Between high school and college relationships, she'd also found ways – conscious or not – to keep herself largely distracted. With everyone away, this was the first stretch of time in a very long while that Loren could recall having entirely to herself. She wasn't on the store schedule for several days, and classes didn't resume until the following week.

She sat on the front steps of the apartment building, reading a book and sipping from a can of beer. She stopped herself at two drinks. She watched TV. She strolled the neighborhood. Once or twice, she walked the campus, where she passed the old haunts, but didn't go inside.

The night before Brooke, Elissa, and Hannah were set to return, Loren stood at The Lookout, gazing out over the falls and smoking a cigarette. When she was first arriving in Grimwood all those years ago, if someone had told her what she would go through over the last few months, she'd have been tempted to take her things and board the next train home.

Of course, if none of it had ever happened, she would never have met Braden. She would never have experienced what it was like to be in a relationship where both people felt they were getting the better end of the deal.

Loren took a final drag on her cigarette as a gust of wind blew the cool spray up from the falls. She brought her hand to her lips and smelled the singed nicotine on her fingertips. She needed to stop smoking. It was beginning to snowball on her.

The coming months would be interesting. She had an impatient, urgent feeling in her gut. She was anxious to get to work, to write and immerse herself in everything she could over the course of the next year.

Loren tossed the cigarette butt over the edge. As she turned on her heel toward town – before she saw him – she knew he would be there, if only for a fleeting moment. Standing in the middle of the square, there and then gone, was Alan Grimwood.

Part 2
Year Four

12.

The sun beat down on the hot asphalt, driving vapor trails from the veins of bubbling tar in the roadway; they swirled around Loren's feet as she ran past. Disgusting as it was, the smell of the tar made her want a cigarette, a maddening craving, as her growing nicotine dependence was the first of two factors behind her newfound running addiction.

The ache in her chest was the second.

Running was Brooke's suggestion. It had gotten her through the worst of things after Jason's death. If it had worked for her friend, Loren figured it was worth a shot as she struggled with her own loss. It was certainly a healthier option than cigarettes and drinking.

Since July, whenever she felt a tingle of temptation, Loren would lace up her sneakers and head out for a run. More often than not, she set out during the heat of the day, punishment by fire. The greater the craving, the harder she pushed herself.

Loren picked up the pace as she passed the bookstore, looking both ways as she stepped off the curb at the next corner. She never turned at 76th, that would take her past Braden's old apartment. Though he was always on her mind, it was vital to maintain a safe distance. If you fed The Black Dog, it might jump up and rip out your throat.

She took a right at the next corner. *This* was where she always made her last big push, shaking the weight from her limbs as she cut over to Greenwood Avenue, pumping her arms and legs, scrambling to outpace every self-destructive thought and impulse. She rounded the corner, whipperwhooling her arms as she slowed to a walk, resting her hands on her waist as she strolled along the front of the building, feeling the edges of her hip bones beneath the sinewy layers of muscle and tissue.

She stretched in the lawn in front of the apartment, feeling the grass and dirt under her fingers. When she'd completed her circuit, and her muscles felt sufficiently appeased, she headed inside.

Loren stripped off her clothes in the empty apartment and strolled into the bathroom, where she looked herself over in the mirror. Though her arm still ached, and her side throbbed at times, physically, she'd never been in better shape. She ran her fingers over her side, once more feeling the edges of the incision. The scar's raised surface had grown smoother, a marker settling uncertainly into the landscape of her skin. Loren turned on the shower and pulled the hairband from her ponytail. When the air was filled with steam, she stepped into the shower to wash the sweat and salt from her skin.

Braden had been gone almost nine months now. It felt like only yesterday, until she realized there would soon be babies born that had not yet been conceived when he was alive.

After her shower, as she was refueling with a bowl of cereal, Loren picked through the mail her roommates had left on the counter for her. Along with the usual assortment of bills and notices from the bursar's office, was a thin envelope from a financial management company in New York. This was the first time she'd received anything from this particular company, but the moment she saw the return address, she knew what it was.

Her stomach tightened with a mix of guilt and anticipation as she tore the envelope open. It was the first check from Braden's attorney. Loren looked from her name to the dollar figure entered in the payment box, and let out an involuntary sigh. Mixed feelings or not, the funds were a relief. She would keep working at the store – that was about more than just money – but this would lift the weight of financial concerns and allow her to focus on the future, without anyone having a say about what she did next.

~

He was gone, but there were always echoes. At the apartment. On campus. All around the store. Corners where she and Braden had discussed books and joked about difficult customers. The spot where she'd seen his face fall when he realized she was with Cole.

For a while, Loren avoided nightshifts at the store, fearing the quiet periods would be the most charged with memories, but over time, she realized that no matter the time of day, no matter what was happening, Braden was *always* there in the moments between customers. He was the reason she worked there in the first place. Books and writing were the threads that drew them together. Eventually, she stopped asking Karl for daytime shifts and started taking whatever hours were available.

"Smoke break?" Karl asked as he bounded down the stairs and held out a pack of Winstons.

Braden had liked Karl, but he would have hated this aspect of the store manager's influence.

"Yeah-" Loren said. "Why not."

They stepped out back and lit up. This had become a regular part of their workdays. A strictly platonic meeting of the minds, philosophical discussions ignited by the Pavlovian smell of freshly lit tobacco as they stood on the back steps, shooting the breeze for the ten to fifteen minutes it took to finish a cigarette.

"School starts up next week, right?"

"Yeah."

"Any shift requests?"

"I'll have to look at my course schedule," she said. "I can't really remember what I signed up for." She'd navigated the last registration period in an understandable haze. "I think I have one or two night classes during the week."

"Just let me know."

Loren drew her cigarette to her mouth and took a long drag as her eyes fell on the red brick building across the way. As always, her gaze settled on Braden's window.

She turned to the store's back parking lot, where another memory bobbed to the surface. Braden standing there in front of his car on that first day back last year.

"Where's your place?" she'd asked him.

"It's right over there." He'd said with a smile as he pointed to his building across the way. "Would you like to see it?"

"Sure…"

"You OK?" Karl asked.

Loren blinked, touching a fingertip to the corner of her eye. "Yeah, I'm fine. Sorry."

"Nothing to be sorry about. It happens to all of us," he said with an understanding smile. "Smoke gets in your eyes."

"What?"

"It's a song."

"Oh, yeah..."

"You sure you're all right?"

She nodded.

"Well," Karl began. "Before we smoke these things down to the filters, let's get down to brass tacks. What are you reading?"

~

Slow Boat to China played hauntingly over the soundtrack as – one page at a time – Famke Janssen threw the only copy of her cheating lover's novel into the waters behind the ferry while Kenneth Branagh watched her boat pull away from the pier at South Street Seaport. As a writer, the site of those floating pages gave Loren a sinking feeling in the pit of her stomach. As a viewer, it triggered an appreciative nod of satisfaction.

The camera lingered on Branagh's face as his shoulder's fell, resigned to the fact that the manuscript for his novel – the only commitment to which he'd remained faithful – was gone. Sitting in the audience at The Little Theater, Loren wondered, not for the last time, what Braden had done with the manuscript for his own novel. It had never turned up, not at his grandfather's house, not in any of the things he'd left at her place, and nowhere in his apartment. Like Braden himself, it had vanished.

~

"That movie was great," Loren exclaimed as she, Brooke, and Elissa walked down the sidewalk after the film screening.

"Totally," Brooke said.

"You know what would be a perfect way to end the night?" Elissa asked.

"Breakfast for dinner at Lola's?" Brooke replied.

"*Exactly.* How did you know?"

"Why would tonight be any indifferent than every other night we've gone to the movies this summer? Hannah is already planning on meeting us there after her class gets out."

~

Hannah looked up from her book with a grin as they arrived at the table. "Have I mentioned how happy I am that I've changed my major?"

"Only the last ten times we've eaten here," Elissa replied.

"Well, I am." Hannah said as she slid her book to the side. "I don't know what I was thinking before-"

"Menus please!" Elissa interrupted, raising her hand to flag down a waitress.

"OK." Hannah said, giving Elissa a look. "Message received."

"Some of us still like architecture, thank you very much, but I'm glad you're happy in the College of Business."

"And *I'm* happy that's settled once and for all," Brooke said, narrowing her eyes at Elissa in a way that said 'that is *that.*'

"What's everybody having?" Loren asked. "I'm getting the usual."

"Same here." Elissa said.

Brooke closed her menu. "Me too."

"I think I'd better eat something lighter than the usual scramble," Hannah mused. "Hank is due back tonight."

"*I'm...* not going to ponder the connection," Elissa said.

"Well, I for one am starving," Loren noted.

"It's all that running you've been doing," Brooke said. "Your body needs fuel."

"Probably." Loren rubbed her arm as she spoke. "It just feels good to move."

"Would you ever think about joining the crew team?" Elissa asked.

"You should!" Brooke added "We've only been practicing for a week. There's still plenty of time to jump in."

"You know, thank you for the offer, but I don't think so. I just like running for me."

"Well, if you change your mind, just let us know," Brooke said.

"Change can be a good thing, Loren," Hannah chimed in.

"Jesus," Elissa joked as she reached for her coffee. "Here we go again!"

* * *

Loren's hair was still wet from her post-run shower as she trudged up the hill to campus. It was freshman move-in day, and the front drive was backed up with cars. Anxious parents were helping their kids unload boxes and checking that they had everything, while self-conscious first year students stood at the curb, trying to look cool while their mothers and fathers put on brave faces and attempted to hold back the tears.

Loren suddenly recalled the auburn-haired girl with the southern drawl who had worked the table the first couple of years, handing out room assignments and keys, while barely giving the newcomers the time of day as she flirted with the procession of frat guys traipsing past. She must have graduated last year. Funny, in Loren's mind, that girl would always be there during orientation, but when she looked over, there was a blond-haired girl in a bright orange shirt manning the table while laughing with a couple of flush-cheeked young frat guys. Time marched on.

Loren picked up her schedule at the bursar's office and headed to the campus bookstore. The place was swarming with students. It took some time, but she finally emerged with her course materials, only to bump into Hank, who was standing by the entrance, drinking a cup of coffee.

"Hi, Loren."

"Hey! You're back."

"I am." Hank motioned to her bag of textbooks. "You've already fought the hordes I see."

"Yeah. If you can avoid it for a while, you'll *definitely* want to wait for things to calm down in there."

"Good to know."

"What are you doing up this early?"

"I don't really know," he admitted. "Hannah was still sleeping, but I woke up kind of wired. Thought I'd get up here, get some coffee, and head over to the station to get my work schedule."

"Can I walk with you for a bit?"

"Of course."

They stepped outside and made their way around the side of the building.

"What are *you* doing up here so early?" Hank asked, as he shielded his eyes from the sun.

"I have a meeting with my senior thesis advisor."

"Already?"

"I'm still making up for lost time."

"I think I know the feeling," Hank said. "I realized doing my co-op this summer that if I *really* want to set up a business like Jason and I talked about, I need to get my shit together *now.*"

"I haven't heard you talk about that in a while. What were you guys going to call your label again?"

"Cradle to the Groove Records."

"Oh yeah. You know, I still don't get that."

Hank rolled his eyes. "*No one* does, but it was Jason's dream, so that's the name."

"Cradle to the Groove it is then. That would make him happy."

"I hope so. Goofy names or not, I still miss that guy." His eyes wandered to the library. "I miss *both* of them."

"Me too," Loren said as she followed his gaze.

"Ever feel like Brady is still in there working?"

"All the time."

~

"I'll be frank with you, your junior thesis… was not the best work we think you're capable of. However, we also know it wasn't completed under the best of circumstances."

Loren pressed her thumb down on the cap of her pen.

She was seated across from Professor Taylor's desk in his den-like office. Everywhere around the room, dark wooden shelves sagged under the weight of hardbound books. Some were arranged horizontally, with other volumes stacked on top. Everything was simultaneously haphazard, yet methodically *just so*. The same could be said for Walter Taylor himself, who looked a bit like Santa Claus, if the old elf worked in a library and only wore pilled, purple cardigans.

Taylor looked over Loren's latest proposal, rubbing his beard in deliberation. As with everything lately, Loren was running a step or two behind, but The Writing Center was working with her to get back on track.

"This is somewhat thin, but I can see where you're going with it," the professor said. "I'd like you to give it another go, but really try to think bigger. Pull it apart, rework it, and let's meet back here again next week to go over it. Sound good?"

~

Sounds good, Loren thought as she stood in the library's shadow after the meeting.

She looked up at the tower's silhouette. She hadn't set foot inside that building since last spring. And yet, it was just like Hank said, anytime she saw the library, she imagined Braden was still inside, hunched over his work.

Now the school year was upon them, cool breezes were cutting through the heat, and she needed to spend time in Braden's world. But a tingle in her stomach told her she didn't just want to see the things Braden knew so well, secretly she was hoping for something more.

Yet, even as she climbed the steps and walked inside, slipping into the season-less comfort and ascending the worn stone stairs, she knew this was a fool's errand. In previous encounters, there had always been a palpable feeling in the air, the weight of mood and emotion that hinted at a realm beyond. Whatever it was – thick and undeniable – today, that sensation simply was not there.

She reached the top of the stairs, passed through the corridor, and entered the paneled room where Braden had always worked. Everything was the same as the last time she'd been there. She strolled down the aisle, past the shadowy alcoves, and once more stopped at Braden's workspace.

He wasn't there.

Why should he be?

Braden was dead and she was alone.

Her neediness and her wish to see him – no matter what that meant for his own happiness and peace – suddenly felt foolish, selfish even.

She was embarrassed. But mostly, she was heartbroken. Time might heal all wounds, but it moved at its own merciless pace. One day, she might learn to accept that.

~

"Did you ever wonder if you'd see Jason again?"

"What?" Brooke asked.

The words had slipped from Loren's lips before she even realized she was speaking. She reached for her beer, her face growing warm, as Elissa looked up curiously.

"I'm sorry, I don't know what made me ask that-"

Brooke pulled her feet up on the couch, hugging her knees as she looked over at her girlfriend. Loren saw their eyes meet, and thought, not for the first time, what a great match they were. There was no jealousy, no insecurity. Before she'd loved Elissa, Brooke had loved Jason, and as far as anyone could tell, each relationship had been just as passionate and strong as the other. Someone less secure might have left the room when Jason was mentioned, but Elissa never batted an eye.

Brooke took a deep breath before she spoke. "I did see him once."

Elissa sat up.

Loren was just as surprised. "When was this?"

"At a crew party sophomore year." Brooke turned to Elissa. "You know the one, where I took those pills with the champagne and cracked my head on the bathroom floor."

Elissa's mouth was flat and tight. "I remember."

It had been a bad scene. Brooke had passed out and nearly suffocated on her own vomit.

"I was unconscious and... *you know*... heartbroken and self-destructive. It felt like I was pulling away, watching everything recede into the distance. And then I saw Jason's face looking down at me. He was peaceful, and calm, but so disappointed. And he said-" She blinked, her eyes darting from Loren to Elissa. "This sounds silly when I say it out loud-"

"No it doesn't," Elissa said. "What did he say?"

"He said 'Don't throw it away, baby.'" She turned to her girlfriend. "Then I heard you banging on the door, and I pulled it together long enough to flip the lock."

"You never told me that," Elissa said quietly. "It's funny, I don't remember much about that night before I opened the door, but I do remember I was talking with someone…"

"Blythe."

Elissa blinked, the corner of her mouth drawing up questioningly.

"I was jealous," Brooke admitted.

"Of *Blythe?* Oh… you *really* didn't have to be."

"And what happened?" Loren asked Elissa. "When you were talking to, you know… this girl we won't name again.

"I had the strangest sensation." Elissa turned from Loren to Brooke. "Like I *had* to put my drink down and go looking for you. It was this nervous energy, like something was pushing me toward that bathroom door. I wish you'd told me that story a long time ago…"

"The only person I ever *almost* told about it was Braden. That New Year's we met up in the city."

"If there was anyone you could talk to about flares, it was Braden." Loren said. "Why didn't you?"

"I guess I was afraid to bring it up." Brooke hugged her legs tighter. "You know what we ended up talking about instead?"

"What?" Loren asked, her throat suddenly dry and tight.

"How much he loved you."

~

Brooke's old lava lamped glowed on the windowsill as Loren lay on her back that night, voices and conversations from the past echoing through thoughts.

"I was talking to Hank today." Braden had said as they lay here in this same bed. *"He said we're in that period with all the firsts…"*

Tomorrow would mark the start of her final year at Grimwood, and the first school year she would begin without Braden. As far as firsts went, this was among the worst.

13.

HAVING DROPPED OUT OF her dream major, Hannah felt more relaxed than she ever had over the previous three years. A longtime aspiration had gone down in flames, yet here she was, making do with a pivot to the College of Business, just about the *last* thing she would ever have imagined herself studying. And even more shocking, all she could see were the pragmatic benefits.

Was this what they called wisdom? Or was she selling out?

She took a seat in the middle row, close to the end of the aisle, and took out her notebook and pen. When she looked up, a familiar plaid shirt and head of brown hair was blocking her view. The student in front of her – an attractive young guy with strong shoulders and a muscular but thin build – was chewing on the end of a pencil, lost in thought. Hannah gently set her hands on his shoulders, leaned forward, and kissed him on the ear.

"Jesus!" Hank exclaimed as he spun around to look at her.

"You didn't tell me you were in this class," Hannah said.

"It never even occurred to me to compare schedules," Hank replied, his expression relaxing as the shock wore off.

Hannah grabbed her things and climbed over the seat to sit down next to him.

"I've never had a class with a lover before," she joked.

"No? They're not bad."

"Oh yeah? You've had a lot have you?"

"One or two." Hank shrugged. "Helps ease the tension."

"Ha. Ha." Hannah replied as she rested her head on his shoulder.

~

Loren dropped her final thesis proposal off before her first class. She felt good about this one. Determined. It was an idea she was willing to fight for. She was still feeling a jittery sense of excitement as she waited for the lecture to begin.

"I see a few familiar faces," Professor Price said as he strolled in and surveyed the room. When he got to Loren he paused and gave her a quiet nod.

As always, Loren immediately looked for a piece of green clothing. Today, it was his necktie. When she and Braden discovered Price's tragic connection to the incident at Grimwood library, they'd come to understand *why* he always wore that color.

"My hope is that this course will resonate with you all now in ways it might not have your freshman year," Price began. "We'll be looking at three writers, and examining works from three different stages of their careers, paying close attention to themes, style, and subject matter, and the ways each of those elements change or *don't change* over the course of their careers. You're at an exciting and nerve-wracking point in your academic careers, where you'll be working on your senior theses, completing your studies at Grimwood, and, assuming we've done our work here, going on to long and illustrious publishing careers. My hope is that it will be helpful at this point to look at those who have gone before you in order to gain some perspective as you look to the years ahead."

~

The quads were swarming with students as the late-afternoon lectures let out. Hank emerged from the school of music, his mind roiling from his new production class. He recognized a familiar figure amongst the sea of backpacks and raced up beside her and took her hand.

Hannah jumped to the side and screamed. "Hank!"

"Fancy meeting you again."

"You scared the hell out of me!"

"Sorry, I thought that was our thing now."

"Consider us even," Hannah said once she'd caught her breath. "How was your recording class?"

"Great. Inspiring and a little overwhelming."

"I *think* that's a good thing, right?"

"Probably."

"I have to confess, I'm a little jealous of you."

"Why is that?" Hank asked.

"You really love what you're studying. You always wanted to do it, and now that you're in the thick of it, it's *still* what you want to do. I wish I had that."

"You will," Hank said. "I mean, look, I'm not studying business because I find it particularly fascinating. I just figure if I want to establish a record label, I need to know enough to keep the thing running without getting robbed blind."

"But you *do* love the music side of things."

"That's true. You've gotta take the bad with the good, right? Eventually you're going to stumble across an idea that brings all of your interests together. Wait and see."

Hannah nodded slowly.

She wasn't ready to say anything yet, but an idea had suddenly occurred to her.

* * *

Hank was seated alone in the gang's customary booth at Bricks when Loren got there. A copy of *The Reporter* – Grimwood's free weekly paper – was spread out on the table before him, opened to the concert page. His shoulders were hunched forward over his mug of coffee, his eyes narrowed as he eaves-dropped on the table behind him.

Loren set her backpack on the bench across from him. "Umm… whatcha doin'?"

Hank raised an index finger to his lips.

Loren took a seat and listened as well.

"So, he killed everyone?" a girl's voice murmured.

"And then he jumped from the top," the boy with her replied.

"How have I never heard about this? When did it happen?"

"I dunno, a *long* time ago."

"Jesus…" the girl grew quiet. "What the heck is a *Brick Plate?*"

Hank winked.

"When was the incident again?" he asked Loren.

"1972." She bobbed her head toward the neighboring booth. "How long were those guys talking about it?"

"Just a few minutes. They seemed to get *most* of the details right. It's strange to hear other people finding out about it for the first time."

"Did you know about it before your first year?"

"A little bit. I knew *of* it. Just the way people always sort of whispered *Grimwood,* like the school and that event were one and the same. Didn't you and Braden have a professor who was dating one of the victims?"

"We did. Mark Price. We even asked him about it once."

Hank choked on his coffee. "Seriously?"

"He was a little taken aback at first, but once he started talking about it, he really opened up. He was clearly still in mourning after all these years. I actually have him again this quarter."

"Does he remember you?"

"I think so, yeah." Loren said. "How are things going?"

"Busy. Two majors and two jobs take up a lot of time."

"And how's Hannah?"

"She takes up a lot of time too," he joked. "We actually have a class together, which is a first. Hopefully she doesn't get too competitive about that."

"Maybe it will be a good thing. I always liked it when I had classes with Braden."

Hank didn't look so sure.

"I guess we'll see how it goes." He began folding up *The Reporter*. "I was just scoping out some bands to check out. I'm thinking of pitching the label for my production thesis."

"Really? What are you proposing exactly?"

"The works. Set up the business. Sign a band. Produce an album. I know I can at least get it a little bit of airtime."

"It's good to be a DJ."

"It's not huge, but every little bit helps, right?"

"Helps what?" Brooke asked as she arrived with Elissa and Hannah in tow.

"Hank is putting the pedal to the metal with his record label."

"Cradle to the Groove?" Brooke asked.

"Yep."

"You know, I've got to build out my design portfolio," she said excitedly. "Do you think I could do your branding and cover design?"

"Absolutely," Hank said. "I was counting on it actually."

Hannah slid into the booth beside Hank. "Let me get this straight. Hank is starting a record label. Brooke is doing all the graphic design for it. Loren, what are you doing for your senior thesis, writing a book?"

"Basically, yeah," Loren said.

"And I'm just starting from scratch again. How depressing."

Elissa raised her hand. "I can tell you what I'm doing if it will make you feel any better."

Hannah studied her for a moment, debating whether or not she wanted to hear the latest developments from the world of architecture.

"What are you doing?"

"I'm writing a journal article studying the legalities and code requirements of septic systems surrounding protected wetlands and coastal flooding regions," Elissa replied.

"Seriously?" Hannah asked.

Elissa nodded.

"That sounds… absolutely horrible." Hannah cracked a broad smile. "That *does* make me feel better!"

14.

HANK WAS LOUNGING ON the dilapidated couch at the back of the sound booth, flipping through the concert listings as he listened to Howard wrapping up his broadcast. Howard's voice was sounding more gravelly than ever these days, like a latter-day Wolfman Jack. Hank closed his eyes and lowered the paper.

"Ow, ow, owhoooooooooo!" Howard yowled into the microphone. "It's six o'clock on a Thursday night, and *this* little minaret is closing down Fort Apache. I need you good people to man the prairie, cause Uncle Howie is reporting for duty at the Pig 'n Whistle!"

Hank opened his eyes and looked around the room with fresh eyes. Howard was seated at the L-shaped broadcast desk, leaning into the microphone. A bank of equipment, lights, and a monitor sat to the right. At the far end of the booth, a large, plate glass window looked into an adjoining room. As always, the room beyond the glass was pitch black.

Hank recalled a long ago conversation he and Jason had had with Howard. He could *still* see his friend's look of wide-eyed excitement when Howard told them what was in that darkened room.

"This is The Rockabilly Bedlam Ball, signing off!!" Howard bellowed into the microphone, then he cut to a recording, pulled off his headphones, and rolled back from the desk.

"Hey Howard-"

"Yeah?"

"You once told Jason and me that if we ever found a band we wanted to record, and we didn't mind a little asbestos exposure, we could do it in there." He pointed to the darkened window. "Is that true?"

"Well, I was joking about the asbestos. I'm pretty sure they'd stopped building with that shit by the time this hovel went up. But yeah, the equipment is as old as time, but it's rock solid, and the acoustics in there are phenomenal. I'd love to see it get some use."

"Awesome."

"At the moment I'm due for a few medicinal Manhattans," Howard said as he hoisted himself out of the chair. "But tell me when you're ready and I can show you how the board and everything in there works." He patted Hank on the shoulder and lumbered out the door.

Hank grinned as he flipped back to the show notices. Just like Jason had imagined all those years ago, Cradle to the Groove would record its first album right here in the studio. Now he just needed to find the right band.

~

A band called The Cellar Bells was playing a late set at The Shack that night. Every review Hank could find for them was stellar. If he flat out ran from the station to the venue after his broadcast, he might be able to catch the last of their set, but he couldn't help but wonder if he should get home and see

Hannah instead. He was still debating what to do when the clouds opened up on the walk to The Ave, drenching him in a sudden downpour.

Hank's clothes were soaked through by the time he got home. He trudged up The Dean's creaking stairs, eager to get inside and get dry, and was already pulling off his coat and sweatshirt as he opened the door to the apartment.

"Hank?" Hannah called from the bedroom.

"Hey," he replied from around the corner as he pulled off his shoes and shirt and stripped out of his jeans. He slipped down the front hall and stopped in the bedroom doorway.

Hannah was sitting in bed reading a management book. She sat up, covering her mouth as she took in his soaking wet appearance.

"You look like Tom Cruise in *Risky Business*…"

"*Oh really?*" Hank asked suggestively.

"…if he'd been dipped in a flea bath." She let out a laugh.

"Well, thanks a whole hell of a lot!"

Hannah got out of bed, still laughing, and ducked into the closet. She reemerged with a towel and started drying Hank's hair.

"I'm sorry. I just wasn't expecting to look up and see you standing in the doorway in your skivvies, soaked to the bone."

"It just started pouring."

"I heard. I was hoping you wouldn't get caught in it, but I'm glad you got home when you did."

"How was your night?"

She gave his hair one last tussle, then tossed the towel away. "It was OK." She leaned in and kissed him. "I was just catching up on some reading before I went to sleep. I was trying to stay up for you though." She gave him another, longer kiss.

"I'm glad you did," Hank said as he put his arms around her.

***

Loren set to work the moment her proposal was approved. She was beginning to understand why Braden had enjoyed his writing time so much. When everything clicked into place, the process was addictive.

It was in that mindset that she eventually decided to try writing in the library as well, smack in the heart of Braden's territory. She wouldn't work in his preferred workspace, that felt like a bridge too far, but she settled instead on a desk tucked into the library's towering columns of iron shelves.

A green banker's light sat atop the small workspace, it's warm glow hitting the pages perfectly as she worked. When she needed a break, Loren would stand and stretch and walk over to the railing to take in the atmosphere of the place.

Over time, she fell into a productive routine between classes and her hours at the store. She wrote new pages in the early mornings, went for long runs through campus and the surrounding streets in the afternoon, and hid away in the shadowy catwalks of the Grimwood Library for late-night editing sessions. To her delight, she was soon turning out page after page of some of the best work she had ever produced, and feeling more inspired and determined by the day.

~

To his surprise, Hank found the first key step in signing a band – namely, walking up and introducing himself – was the most difficult for him. He'd always thought of himself as an outgoing guy, but apparently, having something on the line – real or imagined – threw him off his game.

Tonight was no different as he watched the show from The Baranof's bar. Though he'd planned to approach the band between sets, as time went on and he treated his anxiety with one or two beers too many, Hank lost his nerve altogether. Which was a shame, as it felt like this one was meant to be. The lead singer looked familiar. Even the band name rang a bell somehow.

Asa Flynn and the Fisher Cats.

He knew he'd never seen this particular group play before, but something about them gave him a palpable sense of deja vu. He just couldn't put his finger on why.

The band wrapped their set and Hank set twenty dollars on the bar. He was too toasted to make an effective pitch. They were due to play The Shack the following weekend, perhaps he would make another attempt then.

As he walked out the door, one thought lingered in his mind. *He might not be capable of pulling this off by himself.*

He wished like hell Jason, or *someone*, was around who could do this with him.

~

Brooke sipped a ginger ale as Elissa, Hannah, and Loren cracked open cans of Genesee.

"To our first girls' night," Hannah said. "I feel like we should be sipping rosé or something, not beer."

Loren shrugged. "I like beer."

"Same here," Elissa agreed.

"Is this really our first girl's night?" Brooke asked. "There must have been others, right?"

"Maybe," Hannah said, "but I don't remember them."

Elissa ran her thumb over the condensation on her beer can, "Where did you say Hank is again?"

"Scouting bands."

"It's actually kind of weird not having him around," Brooke observed.

"He's probably happy to have a little time away from all of us girls," Hannah said. "I mean… it must be sort of strange for him to be the only guy now."

"I'm sure it is," Brooke replied as she watched Loren from the corner of her eye. "But he's sort of an honorary member of our little circle. He tries to act all stoic and indifferent, but he's in touch with his feelings too."

"If music is any indication, then yes," Hannah said. "Anyone who can go from Neil Diamond to… I don't know *what* some of that stuff he listens to is called, is definitely operating on some unexpected levels. Of course, that doesn't mean he doesn't act like an absolute *ass* sometimes too."

The girls laughed as Hannah looked around their apartment, at a total loss. "Now, what the hell do we *do* on a girl's night?"

***

"Are you working tonight?" Hannah asked Hank at breakfast

"No, I managed to get the night off."

"From the restaurant *and* the station?"

"Yeah."

"Maybe we should do something then," she suggested. "That hasn't happened on a weekend in… I can't even think how long it's been."

Hank pulled the latest copy of *The Reporter* from his bag and picked up his morning coffee. "I was thinking of going to The Shack to talk to a band tonight."

"Oh yeah?" Hannah asked, trying not to sound disappointed. "How did it go last week?"

Hank sighed. "I choked again. It's harder than I was expecting."

"You just have to be pushy."

"That's easy for *you* to say."

"Oh *is* it?"

"You know what I mean," Hank said. "I've got to get it together tonight though. I think these guys could be perfect."

"Who's playing?"

"A band called The Fisher Cats." He handed her the paper with the page turned to the show announcement. "I realized we actually saw the lead singer a few years back. I don't recognize the other guys, but *The Reporter*'s write-ups have been great."

Hannah read the caption beneath the photo of the band's front man. "Asa Flynn… He's cute."

"Oh yeah? You like that look?"

"I do. I'd play *that* record if you know what I mean."

Hank feigned jealousy as he swiped the paper back. "What are *you* doing tonight?"

"I might see what Loren is up to."

"No Brooke and Elissa?"

Hannah shook her head. "They're headed off on some romantic getaway this afternoon."

* * *

"You haven't been home for Thanksgiving in a long time," Brooke's mother said on the phone.

Brooke held the receiver to her ear as she looked around the apartment. "I know it's been a while. I'm not sure what our plans are yet."

She could almost hear her mother's ears prick up at the word 'our.'

"Oh, are you seeing someone?"

"I didn't know if you and Dad would be in town this year," Brooke said, dodging the question.

"We should be. You're more than welcome to bring someone home for the long weekend. The city is especially romantic around the holidays."

"I'll let you know as soon as I figure out what's happening."

"Just don't wait too long," her mother said. The Lewises are trying to get a headcount for Thanksgiving on the island. I need to tell Susie if we'll be there or if we'll have other plans."

~

"So, where are we headed?" Elissa asked Brooke as they were loading up the car that afternoon.

"Sunset lake."

"Where's that?"

"Somewhere ninety minutes from here," Brooke said. "And *hopefully* a lifetime away from the day to day."

"So dramatic." Elissa said as she gave her a kiss. "You know, I don't think the day to day is all that bad if you want to know the truth."

"I don't either. I just want to go someplace where it's just the two of us for a while. No one else… And no pressure."

~

Someone was having a fire. The smell wafted in through the cracked window above Loren's desk, reminding her of cool autumn nights in Colorado. She closed her eyes, inhaling deeply as she imagined a crackling campfire. She opened her eyes and looked down at her mug of tea. She'd been considering helping herself to Elissa's beer, but she was trying not to have a drink tonight. The morning headaches were getting old, and constantly replacing her roommate's stash had become embarrassing. Plus, even if she managed to get anything down on the page while she was drinking, none of it was ever any good when she went over it the next day with sober eyes. The romance of Hemingway was a lie.

With Brooke and Elissa away for the weekend, and no work on her schedule until Sunday, Loren had an unbroken stretch of time ahead of her, a great opportunity to make some headway on her thesis. She was 180 words into a new story when a knock came at the door.

"Are you busy?" Hannah asked as Loren opened the door. "I was hoping we could hang out."

Loren took a deep breath. "Sure," she said reluctantly.

A few minutes later they were on the couch in front of the TV, flipping through stations in search of entertainment.

Loren hit the mute button as she continued to change channels. "What's Hank up to tonight?"

"He's at The Shack, scouting another band," Hannah said. "Actually, it's the *same* band. He knows he wants to work with them, he just needs to get up the nerve to make his pitch."

"That shouldn't be a problem, right? Hank is perfect for that kind of thing."

"You would think so, right? But he says he keeps chickening out. It's bizarre."

"He's psyching himself out-"

"That's what it sounds like." Hannah agreed.

Loren stopped on a cooking show, where a chef in a large white cap was throwing what appeared to be squid legs into the audience. Meanwhile, someone behind him was dumping alcohol into a frying pan full of tentacles, setting them ablaze in a pyre of flames. Loren's brow furrowed in thought.

"You know, you're pretty pushy, Hannah. Ever think of making the pitches for him?"

"I've been debating that. I'm just not sure if it would go over all that well."

They stared at the TV. Now audience members were rushing the stage, grabbing flaming tentacles in their hands and running around frantically.

Loren's eyes drifted from the onscreen idiocy to the glow of her desk light in the next room. She'd hoped to be knocking out pages by now, but Hannah's unannounced visit had derailed her plans. She was suddenly gripped by the fear that, if she didn't do something now, *this* could be her future. Night after night of interruptions – stretches of prime writing time, repeatedly interrupted as Hannah looked for ways to fill the hours while Hank approached, or *tried* to approach, band after band for his label.

"I think it could be the perfect tactic," Loren said. "Like a tag team Rollins and Joffe approach."

"Who?"

"Never mind."

Hannah started clicking her finger nails on the side table in an accelerating pattern that quickly set Loren on edge.

"OK," Loren said, jumping to her feet when she couldn't take it anymore. "I'm making an executive decision. We should go to The Shack, just to see how it's going."

"You think so? You don't think that will piss Hank off?"

"I'm not saying you have to *do* anything. Just see what's happening, size up the situation, and if it seems like he needs the help, maybe jump in and close the deal."

Hannah flipped off the TV.

"Let's do it," she said as she got to her feet.

Loren was already halfway to the door.

~

Loren followed Hannah through the crowd as the band was wrapping up a number on The Shack's stage.

Hannah arched her neck, peering around the room in search of Hank. She scanned the audience up near the front. No sign of him. She didn't see him at any of the tables either. Just row after row of music fans, holding their drinks, moving to the music, and applauding as the song ended. That left one possibility…

"Thank you very much," the lead singer growled into the microphone. "We're glad you liked it. We've got one more song for you, then we're turning the stage over to Halloqueen for the rest of the night. As for us, we're The Fisher Cats. We hope to see you again real soon."

"Is that the band Hank is here for?" Loren shouted over the noise.

"That's them," Hannah hollered back as she marched toward the bar.

There at the counter, head on his hand, elbow on the bar top, was Hank; a half-empty pint glass sat in front of him.

It took him a moment to register what he was seeing, but Hank sat up as Hannah's face came into focus. "Hey, what are you doing here?"

"I can only do so many girls nights before I get restless," Hannah answered. "So here's the deal. We're here to help. Well, I am, Loren is just along for the ride. How's it going?"

"Hey Loren," Hank mumbled. "It's going OK."

"Did you talk to them yet?" Hannah asked.

Their eyes met.

Hank shook his head. "Not yet."

"Did they take a break at all?"

"Yeah, this is their second set."

"So, then, you've got to talk to them *now*, right?"

"…Yeah."

"Want me to go with you?"

"Why would you do that?"

"Because Loren says I'm pushy."

"Hey," Loren said. "I didn't say it *exactly* like that."

"You said, '*You're pretty pushy, Hannah.*' Did you not?"

"Yeah," Loren agreed uncomfortably, "That sounds about right."

Hank cracked a reluctant smile. "She's right you know."

"I know she is!" Hannah exclaimed as she looked to the stage. The audience was beginning to applaud as the band played its final chords. Then the cheering and hollering began. Hannah had to shout to be heard over the noise of the crowd. "But she also thought I should help you approach these guys, so if you can't get the nerve up in the next two minutes, I'm doing it for you. We might as well put my pushiness to good use.

"I'm doing it. I'm doing it!" Hank shouted back. He drank the rest of his beer, then he caught the bartender's eye and raised his hand, ever so slightly, signaling for another.

The Fisher Cats wrapped their set and stepped down from the stage. The lead singer and two of his bandmates shook hands with some fans as the drummer made a beeline for the backroom.

Hannah stared at Hank. "This is it, babe," she said, jerking her thumb back toward the front of the room. "If you really want to do this , it's now or never."

"Just gimme a second…"

The bartender came over and set a fresh beer on the counter. Before Hank could look up, Hannah took the drink and slid it in front of Loren.

"Clock is ticking Hank, either you go or I go."

"I'm going. I just-"

But Hannah was already on the move, cutting a path through the thick of the crowd.

Hank met Loren's gaze, then he took off after his girlfriend.

Loren stayed behind, considering the beer for a moment. Then she picked it up and took a long swig.

So much for a night without drinking.

By the time Hank caught up to her, Hannah was just approaching the lead singer, who turned to her and smiled.

"Hi."

"Hi," Hannah replied.

"Can I help you with something?"

"Yeah," Hannah said, her mind racing. Whereas Hank seemed to be *over*thinking the process, she hadn't thought it through at all. "Actually, I'm hoping we can help you."

"How's that?" the singer asked. He turned to Hank, hoping for clarification.

Hannah waited for Hank to step in, but when he remained tongue-tied, she barreled ahead. "We're starting a small record label, and we'd like to talk to you and your bandmates about coming on board."

"What's the label?"

"Cradle to the Groove," Hank blurted out.

"Cradle to the Groove," he repeated. "OK… I'm sorry, I didn't get your names…"

Hank put out his hand. "Hank Pierce. This is my partner, Hannah Merritt."

"Asa Flynn," he said by way of introduction. Then he started toward the back room. "Why don't you come on back and give us your pitch."

Hannah shot Hank a look.

Hank swallowed hard. Then he clapped his hands together and clicked into gear. "Let's do it," he said with a grin.

"Great," Asa said as he lead the way backstage.

Hannah exhaled slowly, relieved to see Hank's confidence kick in.

"Good show fellas," Asa announced as he marched into the green room. He pulled three Genesees from an ice filled cooler, handed two of them to his guests, and opened the third for himself.

His three bandmates were stretched out around the room, arms and legs draped over an odd assortment of broken down couches and chairs. They looked up expectantly, wondering who their guests were.

"What's the deal, chief?" The bass player, a guy with thick black glasses and shaggy red hair, asked.

"Folks, this is Hank and Hannah." Asa pointed around the room. "Hank, Hannah, this is Alvy, Woodrow, and Grady."

"Nice to meet you guys," Hank said.

Hannah smiled and raised one hand.

"Have a seat," Asa said as he straddled the arm of one of the couches and pointed toward a pair of folding chairs. He started rehashing the show with his bandmates as Hank and Hannah took their seats. "Alvy, whatever that was you were doing at the start of *Exploding Monkeys,* I loved it."

Hannah looked around the room, trying to put names to faces as they spoke. Other than Asa, the other three were clearly related.

Alvy, the lanky guitar player, had reddish-brown hair and wore round, wire-framed glasses. He seemed to be the most reserved of the three.

Woodrow, the bass player with the black frames was the most muscular member of the group, with thick arms, broad shoulders, and a personality to match. As the conversation went on, he offered the bluntest observations about the show's highs and lows end everything in between.

Then there was Grady – the drummer – who was a little nerdy looking, quiet, and thin. Truth be told, he didn't look like someone who would play in a band... except perhaps Rush.

"Are you guys brothers?" Hannah asked out of the blue. "I know you're not," she said to Asa. "But the rest of you all have a certain look..."

Woodrow laughed and ran his fingers through his hair. "What you're trying to say is that Asa over there is eye candy, and the three of us are homely, but in a similar sort of way."

"That's not what I mean," Hannah said. Her face flushed as she looked at Asa. "I mean, yes, Asa has the lead-singer look going for him, but you three-"

"Clearly don't!" Woodrow laughed again. "It's OK. Don't spare our feelings."

"They're messing with you," Asa said. "But you're right. They're brothers. I'm the outsider."

"How long have you guys been playing together?" Hank asked.

"About two and a half years, off and on," Grady said.

"Before that, they were The Fisher Brothers," Asa said.

"And *he* was in every band under the sun," Alvy added.

"The Fisher Brothers!" Hank snapped his fingers. "A friend of mine *loved* you guys!"

Grady sat up. "What did he say?"

Hank scanned his memory, trying to recall Jason's assessment of the brothers. He remembered plenty of praise for their sound, but some fairly harsh words when it came to the lead singer slash drummer.

Grady waited expectantly.

"Just that you guys… rocked," Hank mumbled.

Woodrow laughed and nodded at Grady. "Did he mention how bad our lead singer was? He did, didn't he?"

Grady's face grew red. This had clearly been a long-running cause for ribbing over the years.

"Not this again," Alvy said. "Give the guy a break. Neither one of us wanted to do it."

"*Exactly!*" Grady exclaimed. He looked at Hank. "I'll admit it though, I was terrible."

Woodrow continued. "We had a review that said we sounded like Mudcrutch if Tom Petty was replaced by a distressed peacock."

"People describe Mick Jagger as a peacock sometimes," Grady said.

"Yeah, but they're talking about his dancing and his clothes, not his voice!"

"Anyway," Alvy interjected, "Once we got together with Asa here, the pieces finally fell into place."

"Yeah," Hank said to Asa. "We saw you once too."

"You and that same friend?" Alvy asked. "How did he describe mister dream pants over there?"

"You reminded us both of a hard-rocking Neil Diamond," Hank said.

Grady burst out laughing. "Neil Diamond. I love it!"

Asa smiled. "I like it. We'll have to meet this friend of yours some day. It sounds like he knows his stuff."

"Yeah," Hank said. "That would be something."

"OK." Hannah clapped her hands together. "Let's get down to brass tacks and see what we can all do together."

~

Loren sat at the bar, working on her third beer as she watched people come and go.

The second band was onstage, working their way through a setlist that did little for her. But to be fair, her mind was somewhat adrift again. Too much beer. Too much time to think.

She was glad they'd shown up to give Hank the push, but she still wished her writing plans hadn't been derailed tonight. Hopefully it was worth the effort, and things were going well backstage. Hank and Hannah had been gone for a while now. That had to be a good sign.

Loren rubbed her head. She was ready to get back to the apartment.

Then she felt a hand on her shoulder, and whipped around to see who was bothering her.

Hannah jumped back, pulling her hand away. "Whoa, you seem a little tense."

"Sorry," Loren said. "I was up in my head. Where's Hank?"

"He's just wrapping things up with the guys."

"How did it go?"

"Really well," Hannah said. "I think they want to work with Hank."

"They want to work with *us*," Hank interjected as he emerged from the crowd and took a seat next to Loren. "Hannah charmed them. They want to meet up again later this week to see what we have in mind."

"That's great!" Loren exclaimed.

Hannah didn't look so sure. "What do you mean they want to work with *us?*"

"You and me," Hank said. "Us."

"What would I do?"

"You'd sign the band, for one thing! I wouldn't even have approached them if you hadn't led the way."

"I don't want to be horning in on your thing, Hank."

"Honestly, if you're interested. I could really use the help."

Hannah still seemed wary of the idea.

"This is a *good* thing," Hank said. "Don't worry so much."

Loren felt funny wedged between the two of them. She was also certain Hannah should help Hank with his plans. With Jason gone, she was the best possible alternative. Before, it would likely have been Jason juggling the production side, while Hank handled the nuts and bolts of the business. Now it would be Hannah minding the Ps and Qs, while Hank focused on their creative endeavors. Somehow, that made perfect sense.

15.

A WEEKEND ON THE lake was just what they'd needed. It wasn't until they got there that Brooke and Elissa realized just how much they'd been craving some time alone. They spent the days hiking, walking along the water, and connecting in front of the fireplace – free of interruptions from Loren, or crew team members, or anyone else. Just the two of them.

The intimacy of the weekend had Elissa thinking about their relationship on a different level. Pondering the future. So it caught her by surprise when they stopped for lunch on the way home, and Brooke seemed to disengage slightly as they sat down to eat.

They were sitting in a booth near the front window of a crowded rest stop diner. A folded table sign tucked between the mustard and the ketchup caught Brooke's eye. It looked like it had been in annual circulation for decades, and showed a little faded cartoon turkey holding up a sign that said, 'Join us for Thanksgiving dinner.'

"This has been a great weekend," Elissa said.

"It has. I kind of hate to go back."

"Is the cabin available tonight? Let's turn around!"

"We both have class in the morning, remember? We'll come back."

Elissa slid her hands across the table, setting them over the top of Brooke's.

Brooke looked her in the eyes and sighed. She glanced at the counter, where a row of diners sat with their backs to them.

"No one is watching us, Brooke."

Brooke pulled her hands away and picked up the menu. "I'm not worried about that."

"Then what's going on? You're acting different."

Brooke didn't answer.

"What is wrong?" Elissa asked louder.

"*Nothing.*" Brooke said sharply.

And the conversation stopped.

A waitress came over, took their orders, and returned to drop off two coffees. And still they didn't speak.

The quiet stretched on through their meal.

Brooke didn't say anything, and Elissa didn't try to break the silence.

They ate, paid for their meal, and got back on the road without another comment.

It wasn't until they were approaching the outskirts of Grimwood that Elissa again said something. "Brooke, what is it? If you're conflicted about anything here, I want to know about it *now* before we get into this any deeper."

That broke the quiet.

"Can we pull over?" Brooke asked.

"Will you talk to me then?"

"Yes." Brooke said, her eyes glistening.

Elissa pulled into a lot, put the car in park, and looked at Brooke expectantly.

"I'm sorry, I wasn't trying to be rude," Brooke said. "I'm not conflicted about anything, or doubting us. It has nothing to do with any of that."

"Then what is going on?"

"I spoke to my mother on the phone before we left. It's been in the back of my mind ever since. I kept meaning to talk to you about it, but we were having such a nice weekend that I was reluctant to bring it up." She rubbed her eyes. "Look, you haven't met my parents. No one I've ever been with, other than Jason, has really ever met them. And they were sort of awful to him. Anyway, my mother was asking about Thanksgiving before we left, and I saw that holiday flyer on the table and remembered that I haven't..."

"You haven't told them about me," Elissa said.

"I've talked *about* you, I just haven't really explained... us. This."

"This," Elissa repeated. "I thought you had settled all of *this.*"

Brooke looked confused. "What do you mean?"

"I mean, I've been with people who haven't been open with their families, who wanted to keep everything secret. I've ridden that rollercoaster, and I don't want to buy another ticket-"

"Elissa-"

"-because you never seem to get off."

"Elissa, that's not what's going on here. I have no problem telling my parents about our relationship, not because of who we are or aren't. I don't give a shit about that. *They* might be uncomfortable, but that's their problem. I don't want their approval. I don't need it."

"Then what's the problem?"

"I don't want them spoiling this. I'm afraid their voices will get in my head, or worse, get in *your* head, and get us all twisted up. And I don't want that happening. You're too important to me. They're superficial people. Their values and what they want out of life – they just don't make sense to me."

"Is that why you got so distant?"

"Yeah, I just got overwhelmed thinking about it all of a sudden. I'm sorry."

"So, I think that settles it," Elissa said.

"Settles what?"

"We need to go to the city and spend Thanksgiving with your folks."

"Why?"

"If just the *idea* of it gets you so wound up that you can't even talk to me about it, then that is something that needs to be addressed head-on."

Brooke reached over and took Elissa's hand. "I'm warning you, they can be real dumbasses."

Elissa shrugged. "Dumbasses can be amusing."

"They can be infuriating."

"Either way," Hannah said. "I think we need to go."

* * *

"All right, what's the plan of attack?"

"Attack?" Hank lowered his coffee. "How about we just talk to them?" Hannah looked around Brick's, rubbing her hands together impatiently. "You don't think we need to make a certain impression? Fake it til you make it, that sort of thing?"

"I don't think there's any faking it here. As soon as I tell them where we're planning to record the album, the jig will be up. They need to be cool with things being a little unconventional at the start. We just need to be enthusiastic and committed."

"Or fit to be committed," Hannah laughed.

"That too," Hank said as he spotted Asa and the guys heading their way.

"What's up, folks?" Asa said as he took a seat.

The brothers slid into the booth as well.

"You guys come to Brick's a lot?" Hank asked.

"A bit," Alvy said. "More when I was in school here."

"You went to Grimwood?" Hannah asked.

"I did," Alvy said.

"Alvy and Woodrow *both* did," Grady added. "They're trained electrical engineers."

"Seriously?" Hank asked. "How the heck did you end up playing music then?"

"That's his doing." Woodrow pointed at Grady, who just laughed.

"I'm a bad influence," he said.

Hannah studied the Fisher brothers, That made sense, Alvy and Woodrow both had the look of vintage Grimwood engineering graduates. Slight frames. The glasses. They were both quiet and borderline nerdy. They reminded her a bit of Jason actually. The third brother, Grady, was built like a gorilla, with big arms, a broad chest, and a mechanic's hands.

On the other end of the spectrum was the only non-Fisher in the band. Asa looked to be in his early thirties, with chiseled features, long, blond hair, and tattoos running up his toned arms. Whereas the brothers were your classic rock and roll outliers – Asa was one hundred percent frontman, with the looks, confidence, and voice to match.

"What'll you have," Betty asked. She gave each of the brothers a no-nonsense once-over, but lingered on Asa just a half-beat longer.

Everyone ordered Brick Plates, including Hannah.

"What the hell?" she said. "Whatever happens, the night will be memorable, right?"

"So, why should we go with you guys?" Grady asked. "What do you have to offer?"

"You'll have to excuse our brother's blunt approach," Woodrow said.

"It's a fair question," Hank replied. "The truth is, we're just getting started-"

"So our biggest selling point is passion," Hannah said. "Let's just be upfront about this. We're a strictly seat of our pants operation. We're talking chicken wire and bailing string. We have no office, no contacts, no recording studio-"

"Whoa, whoa, hold up," Hank interrupted. "My girlfriend is casting an overly transparent and bleak picture. What she means to say is that we're hungry, we're enthusiastic, and we're *driven,* so you're going to get everything we can possibly give to this project."

"What's this about not having a studio?" Asa asked. "I was under the impression you wanted to cut a record with us. Do you have *any* recording space available?"

"Not a studio per se," Hank admitted. "But we have access to a *kind* of studio."

They stared at Hank and Hannah blankly.

"And you have guys to run it?" Alvy asked.

"We have *a* guy," Hank offered. "Me. And Hannah as backup of course."

The band exchanged wary looks.

"And where *is* this?" Asa asked.

Hank filled him in on the station's recording booth. "It's old technology, but I think it could be amazing. Dave Grohl has recorded on this type of board numerous times. It's a treasure."

"Once Hank is trained to use it, it's going to be gravy," Hannah added.

"You don't even know how to *use it?*" Woodrow asked. "When are you going to learn?"

"This Saturday. Howard is going to come in and show me the ropes."

"Howard…" Asa murmured.

The brothers sighed.

Betty brought over their Brick Plates, distributing them in the quiet of deliberation.

"I'll be honest with you," Asa said finally, "We've had some interest from a couple of small, but much more established labels over the last year, but we've held off, for fear of them tripping us up. As far as this proposal is concerned, it's the least enticing for a lot of reasons. Lack of funds, no company history, no resources of any kind, except for a non-studio and some guy called Howard. But you seem driven."

"Driven enough to sign on the dotted line and give us a chance?" Hannah asked, pushing her luck to the breaking point.

Asa looked around the table at his bandmates. After a long pause, they all nodded. "What the hell?" he said. "If it all goes to hell, at least we'll get a story out of it."

"Or a lawsuit," Grady noted.

Hank and Hannah exchanged nervous glances.

~

Hannah was charged up on the walk home, rattling off the list of things they needed to do as she did a sort of boxer's shuffle down the sidewalk.

"We're going to need to set up some business paperwork. And you need to get trained on that machine. And we need to talk to Brooke about getting some design mockups together ASAP."

"Before any of that, I need to get a proposal into the department for this whole endeavor," Hank noted. "Can you help me with that too?"

"Absolutely," Hannah said. "We'll get this up and running and knock it out of the park, or whatever analogy works for this. It's going to be-"

"Hannah?"

"Yeah?"

"Thank you."

She looked pleasantly surprised. "You're welcome."

"It's nice to have someone working on this with me again. I'm glad it's you."

"I'm glad it is too," Hannah said.

16.

At the end of a *particularly* solitary day, Loren found herself walking on the cold brick campus pathways, with no particular destination in mind. Her eyes blinked slowly against the cold. The wind whipped her hair. And soon enough, she knew where she was headed. To the library to work on her thesis.

Leaves swirled at the entrance, riding the draft through the doors as she ducked inside the library. The heat and quiet enveloped her, seeping into her bones as she made her way through the library. Loren climbed the spiral stairs, crossed the catwalk above the main floor, and stopped at her workspace of choice. She flipped on the banker's light, its warm glow illuminated the desktop as she set out her notebooks, took a seat, and slipped into her work.

At some point that evening, Loren looked up from the pages and saw a familiar figure pass by. Though she caught but the briefest glimpse, the features were unmistakable.

Loren calmly rose to her feet, walked to the end of the aisle, and, finding that he had already slipped out of sight, set off in search of him. She passed row after row of books, climbing stairs and peering around shelves, until she arrived once more at Ashton Study Hall. It was, as always, quiet and deserted as she walked down the aisle and stopped at the usual workspace.

And there, as she knew he would be, was Braden.

He turned and smiled, his movements ever so slightly slower than she remembered. "Why aren't you working in here?" he asked.

"It's too hard, Braden." Her eyes shimmered. "I had to find my own place."

"It's sure peaceful though. I'm glad you're writing."

"Finally, right?"

He smiled reassuringly.

"How long have you been here?" Loren asked.

Braden blinked, the movement seeming a step or two out of sync with the space around him. "I don't really know," he said. "Sometimes I'm here. Sometimes I'm not. It's like a daze. I'm in my thoughts, but there's only darkness. Then I open my eyes, and I'm back here, working."

"Of course you are…" Loren smiled and wiped away a tear. "Making the rest of us look bad."

They studied one another's faces.

"I miss you, Loren."

"I miss you too. Like crazy."

"I'm always around, just between the lines."

"Now you're trying to sound all literary."

"Yeah, I am." He smiled, the corners of his eyes crinkling the way she remembered. "How is everybody?"

"They're good. Hank and Hannah are doing so much better. He's starting his record label."

"That's great."

"Brooke is totally in love."

"She deserves it," Braden murmured. "And how are you?"

Her eyes were filling. "I'm writing. That's the important thing, right? Working it out on the page."

She told him more about her thesis.

"So, it's a collection of stories that tie together like a novel…"

"Hopefully," she said. "But I'd *still* like to finish the year with a traditional novel in the bag."

"Like our baby, right?"

"Yeah," she whispered, remembering their abandoned collaboration.

"You're going to do it, Loren. I know you will."

* * *

"I saw him."

Brooke looked up from the bag she was packing for her Thanksgiving trip to the city with Elissa. "Saw who?"

"Braden."

"What do you mean you saw him? Like…?"

Loren nodded. "Do I sound crazy?"

"Not to me. I told you about Jason, remember? Where was this?"

"The library. I've been going there to work lately. The truth is I'd sort of half-heartedly wondered if I might see him at some point, but I never *really* expected it to happen. Only today felt different somehow. There was a mood in the air, like I could almost *sense* him, and then he was just… there."

"And what happened?"

"We talked. Like it was a perfectly natural thing."

"You spoke? When I saw Jason, I could just hear him in my head, like someone calling from another room."

"We had a conversation. Just the same as always. Unless I dreamed it."

Brooke shook her head. "I don't think it was a dream."

"I don't either."

"Do you think you'll see him again?"

Loren was quiet, once again picturing Braden's slowly blinking eyes.

"I hope so."

* * *

The train ride down to the city was peaceful. Elissa peered out the window at the passing towns, while Brooke sketched ideas for Hank's album cover. Then she rested her head on Brooke's shoulder, and eventually fell asleep.

She awoke in Grand Central Station.

"We're there, baby," Brooke said as she gently shook Elissa's shoulder.

Elissa looked up at the ceiling of painted stars as they emerged in the main concourse.

Brooke glanced over at the split-flap boards as they began cycling through the schedules. She cracked a wistful smile.

"What is it?" Hannah asked.

"I was just remembering meeting up with Braden at this exact spot years ago. I'd forgotten all about it."

Then they were out on the streets, walking up Fifth Avenue, taking in the sites of New York at Thanksgiving. The tree at Rockefeller Center. The shop windows bursting with extravagant holiday displays.

"What do you think?" Brooke asked as they passed The Plaza.

"I love it," Elissa said. "Where are we off to next?"

"Well, I think we've put it off as long as possible. We might as well head over to my parent's place."

"Where is that?"

"They're on the Upper East Side. We've still got a little ways to go."

"Lead the way."

~

"So, I take it Cathie isn't coming?" Hannah said as she pulled an assortment of prepared Thanksgiving dishes from the Wegman's box.

"I left her a message," Loren said. "But I haven't heard anything."

Hank uncorked a bottle of wine. "Who wants vino?"

Both girls raised their hands.

"I can't say I blame her for wanting to move on," Loren said. "Plus, she's the closest with Brooke, so it would have been a little awkward with just us."

"The losers…" Hank said as he filled their glasses. "I wouldn't hang with us either."

"Well, we *are* eating a precooked grocery store dinner," Hannah noted.

Hank shrugged. "Why should we waste an entire bird? This way we can relax, put on some records, and scheme."

"Makes sense to me," Loren said. "What are we scheming about?"

Hank and Hannah exchanged looks.

"Should we tell her?" he asked.

"Tell me what?"

"Hank signed his first band."

"The guys we saw at The Shack?"

Hannah nodded. "We're recording the album over the Christmas break.

"Howard has been showing me how to use the old setup at the station. It's this awesome piece of equipment that no one knows is there. The album should sound amazing if we can pull it off."

"That's awesome! Let me know if I can help."

"You can help," Hannah said immediately.

"Hannah is helping me get the label up and running, including the recording of this first album."

"What do you need me to do?"

"I don't know yet," Hannah replied. "But trust me, we'll need all the backup we can get. It's going to be a marathon recording session."

"We're gonna do it over the Christmas break so we have minimal chance of interruption," Hank explained. "The studio space is all ours, we just can't interfere with the day to day radio schedule."

"Personally, I think we could just put The Chipmunks on repeat for twenty four hours," Hannah said. "But it's apparently more involved than that."

"Just a bit," Hank confirmed. "I'm thinking of prepping as much on tape ahead of time as I can, but even then, it's going to be a balancing act."

"Well, sign me up," Loren said.

"You're not going home for break?" Hannah asked.

Loren shook her head. "I don't think it's going to be much of a Christmas. It sounds like my parents are finally calling it quits."

"I'm sorry to hear that," Hank said.

Loren didn't look so upset. "It's been a long time coming, but I'd rather not make the 2,500 mile trip back there for two weeks of melodrama."

Hannah raised her glass. "Why do that when you can join us for two weeks of high drama instead?"

~

Elissa grew unusually quiet as the elevator ascended to Brooke's parents' place. They stepped off in the hallway outside the apartment door and waited for the elevator to close before Brooke said anything.

"Look, I hope I didn't scare you too much about my parents," Brooke said as she fished out her housekeys. "They can be weirdos, but they're not bad people."

"I'm fine," Elissa reassured her. "You don't need to worry about me."

"Are you sure?"

Elissa nodded and gave her a kiss. "Open the door already."

Brooke took Elissa's hand as they walked inside.

"Mom, we're home."

"Brooke!" her mother called from the next room.

They were still holding hands when she came around the corner. Brooke watched her mother's eyes as she noticed their intertwined fingers. Then, in a moment Brooke hadn't expected, Cristina Winston smiled and moved on.

"I've been waiting for you two to get here," she said as she gave Brooke a hug. She turned and hugged Elissa as well, holding her arms around her a moment longer than she'd held her own daughter. "Elissa, it's very nice to meet you."

"Thank you for having me," Elissa said.

"I was just about to have a late lunch if you girls wanted to join me," Cristina said as she led the way into the kitchen.

Brooke gave Elissa's hand a squeeze as they followed behind.

~

Brooke's father returned home later than expected. The sky was dark, and the apartment was filling with the smells of turkey as they took their seats at the dining room table. Brooke heard the old familiar sound of the front door opening, and her father's briefcase dropping on the floor at the bottom of the stairs.

"I'm home," he announced bluntly.

Cristina excused herself and slipped out into the foyer.

The caterer came in from the kitchen with their plates of food.

"Thank you," Brooke said as the first plate was placed in front of her.

She looked over at Elissa as a plate was placed before her as well.

Brooke had an inkling of what was happening in the next room. Her mother was telling her father a bit of news; that the friend Brooke had brought home for the holidays was more than just a friend.

When her father emerged in the doorway, the smile on his face, and the way he came over to Elissa straight away, made Brooke appreciate her mother more than she'd ever thought possible. She didn't know what was going on with her parents, but they were clearly making an effort. Perhaps spending so some much time away from home had put some things in perspective for them a bit. She wouldn't hold her breath from here on out, but so far, she was very pleasantly surprised.

~

Loren walked home alone, wary of the quiet waiting for her in the empty apartment. Thanksgiving had been good. As good as possible, considering she'd been the fifth wheel at Hank and Hannah's place.

She helped herself to one of Elissa's beers when she got home, drinking it in the shower before she slipped into her pajamas and climbed into bed. Then she lay in the darkness, listening to the creaks and pops as the building settled in the cold.

The holidays were coming up fast now. It was jarring to think of how much had changed in less than a year. It would be good to have the recording sessions as a distraction. Something to keep her mind in the present.

17.

Loren arrived at work the next morning to find that Christmas had crash-landed at R. K. Phillips books. Garland, lights, and greenery were scattered everywhere as Karl led a team of booksellers through high speed holiday preparations, even as the first shoppers of the season were arriving with their shopping lists in hand.

Apparently, there'd been some miscommunication over who was responsible for the holiday decor. Karl thought one of the floor merchandisers was in charge of decking the place out in time for Black Friday, but Roxanne had been expecting *him* to have all the decorations in place by the time the doors opened. When she arrived at 7 a.m. that morning to find the store completely bare, all hell had broken loose.

"No one appreciates segues," Karl muttered as he and Loren snuck a smoke in back. "They want everything to be like a Daffy Duck cartoon. Zip, he's dressed in a bullfighter outfit. Zip, he's in a suit of armor. Boom, Halloween decorations everywhere. Bam, Thanksgiving crap everywhere. Oop, now it's Christmas."

"What does Daffy Duck have to do with this?"

"You know, like *Duck Amuck…* with all the quick changes."

Loren look at him blankly.

"You don't know *Duck Amuck?* That really great Chuck Jones cartoon?" He looked genuinely perturbed. "Anyway, it's a classic. Come to think of it, Roxanne reminded me a little of Daffy when she was handing me my head this morning."

Loren laughed and glanced through the café window into the store. "We'd better get back to work before it happens again."

"No kidding," Karl agreed as his mashed his cigarette out.

They walked back inside, the bell on the door jingling behind them as they returned to the sales floor. Easy listening Christmas music was now playing through the sound systems. A massive box of artificial garland came walking around the corner toward them.

"Perfect timing," Karl said to the greenery. "Loren here is going to help you finish up the decorations.

The box of garland pivoted, and Loren recognized a longtime coworker who had left at the end of August for her first year at NYU.

"Virginia! When did you get back?"

Two days ago," Virginia responded.

"And you're already back at the store?"

"New York isn't cheap. I have to make some money wherever I can."

By late afternoon, the bookstore looked as though it had been undergoing holiday preparations for weeks. Virginia was at the top of a ladder, weaving garland around the overstock books, when she looked down and muttered something under her breath. Loren couldn't quite make out her words, but Virginia's disdain was palpable.

"What is it?" Loren asked.

Virginia motioned, and Loren turned around to find Cole Phillips standing behind her. A tall brunette, with thick makeup and a kicked-in-the-forehead daze about her was standing beside him, studying a coffee table photography book. Cole was looking at Loren from the corner of his eye, and smiled warily when they made eye contact.

"Cole."

"Hey, Loren," he said. "The place is looking good. I feel like I should be working on that with you."

She gave him a confused look.

"Putting up the decorations was sort of our thing, remember?"

Loren flashed to a long-ago image of Cole wearing a wreath on his head like a crown as they decorated the store. That was back before they'd even dated. Braden had openly disliked Cole even then, and it had caught Loren by surprise when she started developing a crush on him in spite of herself.

"I'd forgotten all about that." Loren said.

"Forgot what?" Cole's companion asked.

He indicated the decorations. "We used to do this together years ago."

"Oh," she said, disinterested, and went back to her photo book.

Loren studied Cole's date curiously, until he made the introductions. "Amber, this is Loren. Loren, this is my fiancé Amber."

"Nice to meet you," Loren said.

Amber seemed annoyed by the interruption. "Hi."

"When's the big day?" Loren asked.

"We haven't decided yet," Cole said. "Sooner than later, hopefully."

"Where did you meet?"

"Saint Tropez," Cole said.

"Well *that's* not too shabby."

"My father keeps a home outside Antibes," Amber said without looking up. "We go there each year for Cannes, and stay for a week afterward to unwind."

"I've heard the festival is *quite* the ordeal." Virginia chimed in.

Cole looked from Amber to Virginia, picking up on the sarcasm, but choosing to ignore it.

"You have *nooooo* idea," Amber replied grimly.

"Anyway, we met at this beautiful restaurant right there on the beach," Cole said. "I had proposed by the end of the weekend, didn't I?"

Amber turned the page, but said nothing.

Cole bobbed his head in the silence, meeting Loren's gaze.

"I was sorry to hear about Braden."

"Thank you."

"He hated my guts, but I thought he was a good guy."

"Thanks. He didn't hate your-"

"Yeah he did," Cole interrupted. "But that's OK."

"How long are you in town?"

"Just until tonight. Amber and her mother have some big shopping plans for the weekend."

Loren nodded.

Follow-up questions were hard to come by.

"We better finish decorating before your Mom gets back. It was good seeing you Cole."

"You too," he said.

They exchanged a gentle hug.

"Amber, congratulations."

Amber looked up, gave a delayed nod, and absentmindedly dropped the book in her basket as she strolled away.

"I'm not sure which one is making the bigger mistake," Loren said once Cole and fiancé were out of sight.

"Really?" Virginia replied. "I think they're a perfect match,"

"Maybe you're right." Loren said.

In a funny way, it had actually been sort of nice to see Cole Phillips again. Loren had absolutely no interest in him anymore, but she could still see what had attracted her to him years ago. She was also greatly relieved that she would not be the one to end up with him for the long haul, assuming he and the awful Amber ever set a date and closed the deal.

***

"I like it!"

Hank held Brooke's mockups at arm's length to get a better look. They'd decided to make the cover image and the record label's logo one and the same, so the first record would announce the band's debut as well as the arrival of Cradle to the Groove Records. It was all done in a sort of Charles Addams meets Edward Gorey illustration style, depicting an upright casket beneath the ground, with a half-submerged record acting as a tombstone, and a carefully-placed grave marker in the background giving the whole thing the look of a ghoulish, half-buried baby bottle. Off to the sides, skeletal hands were digging through the worm-riddled soil, reaching for the casket.

"I knew you were a designer, Brooke, but I had no idea you were this *good.*"

"Thanks... I think. I was thinking of adding a dancing skeleton inside the box, but I wasn't sure if it would be too much. "

"Could we try it both ways, see how it looks?"

"Absolutely. It will take a little more time, but if you don't need me for every minute of the recording sessions, I can definitely try it both ways."

Hank called into the kitchen, where Hannah was busy working out the schedule. "Hannah, does that sound do-able?"

"Yeah, we can do that. Between you, me, Loren, and Elissa, we should be able to man the controls and keep the show going at the same time.

"Show?" Brooke asked.

"Slight monkey wrench," Hank explained. "Turns out I'm scheduled to run the station every night we're planning to record next week."

"That should be interesting. Is that even *possible?*"

"It'll have to be, right?"

18.

The University shut down for break one week before Christmas, but the town was still bustling with shoppers and local kids returning home for the holidays. With the recording sessions looming, the gang was sticking around for the season. The others had spent multiple holidays in Grimwood, but this would be Hank and Hannah's first Christmas in town. With the anniversary of the accident fast approaching, Loren welcomed the distraction. There was something comforting in the five of them circling the wagons and spending their final Christmas at Grimwood, working on Hank's project together.

It was going to be busy though. The station would be closed on Christmas, so they had to record the album in four days, a condensed timeframe that grew even tighter when Hank learned he was scheduled to deejay the bulk of the broadcast hours over that same period of time. That meant he'd have to run the soundboard *and* oversee the airwaves simultaneously. In hopes of minimizing the chaos, he was in the process of teaching Hannah how to juggle a series of prerecorded intros and outros, but it remained to be seen how that would play out.

Loren relished the bustle of activity as she worked back to back shifts at the store – wrapping presents, staffing the sales floor, and even manning weekday author events. The atmosphere was hectic but strangely invigorating.

Once the recording sessions got underway, Loren began running to the station at night to lend a hand as Hank and Hannah worked with the band. She arrived at the studio late the first night, as Hank was showing Hannah how to cut to the tape, and Asa and the band were setting up their equipment in the next room.

Hank and Hannah were hunched over the broadcast desk, the microphone pushed to the side as Hank cued up a tape recording and swung the microphone around. He silently drummed his finger on the edge of the desk in time with the countdown, then pointed at Hannah, who hit PLAY to run his intro.

"Stick around for another set of your favorites," Hank's recorded message announced. *"And stay tuned to WGRM!"*

Hank waved his hand, trying to catch Hannah's attention. When she saw what he was pointing at, she reached over and hit STOP. Then she flipped another switch, and the broadcast cut to the lineup of songs Hank had already preprogrammed.

"Not bad," he said as he headed into the next room. "The next one isn't due for 30 minutes, let's start a timer and check on the guys."

Hannah set a timer on her watch and looked up.

"How's it going," Loren asked.

"I think I'm getting it," Hannah sighed. "But I may need some help."

"Are Brooke and Elissa coming?"

"They should be back with the pizzas soon. What's it like out there?"

"Cold," Loren said. "The temperature is definitely dropping."

~

The snow started rolling in as they were making their way to Red Tomato.

"I'm glad we're all together," Brooke said, "but I wouldn't mind being somewhere warmer for the holidays next year."

"Like where?" Elissa asked.

"Maybe we could go out to Tacoma together after graduation."

"I like the sentiment," Elissa said, "But just so you know, Tacoma isn't much different than here. Less snow, but if anything, it's grayer and wetter. Then again, it *is* just one flight away from Maui."

They reached Red Tomato and ducked inside.

"Let's go to Maui then," Brooke said.

"*That* I could be down for," Elissa said. "How many pies are we picking up, again?"

"Six I think."

Victoria, a tall, blonde girl who they'd met once before, emerged from the back. "How can I help you?" she asked.

"We're picking up an order for Hank Pierce," Elissa said.

Victoria smiled, "Ah Hank. Just one second."

"I do like that St. Pauli Girl," Elissa murmured as Victoria slipped into the back.

"Oh stop," Brooke said, giving her a little shove. "And I believe her name is *Victoria*, not 'that St. Pauli Girl.'"

"So, brass tacks, are you serious about Tacoma? Cause I'd love to move back after graduation, but I'm open to anything. I just want to stick together, if you're up for it."

"*Of course*. Just as long as you keep your eyes off folks like Victoria"

"I saw you looking too," Elissa whispered.

"Hank!" A voice called.

They turned to see Hank's boss, Elaine – a heavily made up woman with jet-black hair – emerge from the back with a pile of pizza boxes in her hands. "This is the big day right? The first day of recording."

"That's right," Brooke said.

"Well I hope this keeps everyone fed." She hoisted the boxes on the counter, then leaned down and brought up a couple of large paper bags. "We threw in some extras, and plenty of breadsticks and soda."

"That should do the trick," Elissa said. "How much do we owe you?"

Elaine waved her hand dismissively. "For Hank? It's on the house."

"Are you sure?"

"Just tell him we love him," Victoria added. "And to make a good record."

"We'll do that," Brooke said. "Thank you so much."

"Let us know if you need more," Elaine said. "We'll have it ready."

Brooke and Elissa juggled the boxes and bags and headed out the door. "That was so nice of them."

"Are you going to tell Hank Victoria loves him?" Brooke asked as they started for the station.

"Hell no! Not in front of Hannah I'm not!"

~

Hannah yawned and led the way into the broadcast booth. "Let me show you how to cue up the next program block, then I'm gonna try to get some sleep.

"Hey, folks. I'd like to take one more stab at that track," Hank said to the band from behind the mixing board as the girls walked through. "I want to try another take and loop it in like Alvy was suggesting."

Hannah's watch buzzed and everyone turned her way. "That's the three minute warning," she said to Loren. "I'd better get you up to speed on this harebrained operation of ours before I crash."

Once she'd been shown the ropes, Loren helmed the airwaves for the next six hours, playing Hank's prerecorded intros at the top of every hour before cutting to the music. She thought she'd done a pretty good job overall, but around 3 a.m., she could feel the fatigue getting the better of her. She wasn't positive, but she thought she might have accidentally repeated one of the announcement tapes around 4 a.m., but no one said anything. By 5 a.m., Loren's vision was beginning to blur. By the time she handed the desk back to Hannah, she was really dragging. That didn't bode well for another full day's shift at the shop.

"How did it go?" Hannah asked.

"Good overall," Loren said before mentioning the possible double-play.

"I think I've done the same thing." Hannah laughed. "Are you going to be OK for work?"

"I guess I have to be," Loren said." I'm gonna head to the apartment, take a shower, guzzle a pot of coffee, and get back to selling books to the holiday crazed masses. How about you?"

"Assuming no-one hits the wall, we'll just be recording."

~

Loren completed her latest shift around nine o'clock that night, and stopped at DiBellas on the way back to the station to pick up Hank's order of subs for the band.

Hank's voice was coming from the speakers in the lobby when she arrived at WGRM. He was introducing a string of rockabilly tracks. Yet, when Loren passed the actual recording booth, she saw Hank and Hannah lying on the floor, sound asleep. Asa Flynn was passed out on the couch a short distance away. The brothers were also unconscious.

Loren looked to the broadcast booth and saw Brooke and Elissa slumped at the desk. Brooke had her arm draped around Elissa's shoulder. Elissa opened one eye and gave a weary thumbs. Loren tossed the bag of sandwiches on the table, staggered across the room, and fell asleep on the floor with the rest of the group for a few hours rest.

The long days had finally caught up with everyone.

~

"I think it's coming out great," Hank said as he leaned his head against the back of the restaurant booth. "If we push it, we can probably get the bulk of the recording done tonight."

"You hear that, Grady? Don't overdo it on the Brick Plate," Asa cautioned.

"Too late," Woodrow said as he noted his brother's cleaned plate.

"Give me a break, will ya?" Grady grunted. "Why is everyone always picking on *me?*"

"I really don't know," Alvy admitted. "But it brings us together."

After reaching an incapacitating level of fatigue and hunger, the group had finally decided to take a break and venture out into the snow for their first hot meal in days. Everyone was looking very much the worse for wear. Especially the members of the band, who hadn't been able to slip away for showers or anything in the way of personal care for days, and were quickly returning to their bearded ZZ Top roots as a result. In short, they were a jarring sight amidst the bustling Christmas Eve atmosphere at Brick's.

Hannah patted Grady on the shoulder. "If it makes you feel any better, I think they pick on you too much too-"

"Thank you, Hannah."

"-but seriously, go easy on the Brick Plate, the grease and all that drumming can't be a good combo."

The group broke into laughter as Betty came over with a round of eggnogs.

Asa stood at the end of the table, brushed the hair from his eyes, and hoisted his drink overhead to make a toast. "Folks, I can't think of anywhere I'd rather be right now, other than here, on Christmas Eve, with the bunch of you, making this album. Well, I guess I can think of a few places… Maui. In the hands of an attentive groupie. Maybe a ski lodge in Vermont. In the hands of an attentive groupie…"

"Oh shut up, will ya!" Grady shouted.

"Seriously though, this has been great. I think I speak for all of us when I say it's been a lot of fun working with the bunch of you, seeing what Hank can do with our tracks, and racing against the clock to put this album together. It's been a real high point for me…"

"Except for that time with that attentive groupie, right?" Alvy said.

"Except for that," Asa agreed. "But seriously, I just wanted to thank all of you for your hard work. And looking at the clock, it appears we're about twelve hours away from Christmas, let's see if we can finish this record!"

~

For Brooke, watching Hank collaborate with the band felt in a way like she was seeing Jason's long-ago dream become a reality. She felt lucky to be a part of it.

She'd tried calling Cathie Pepper the previous week, but just as it had all year, her call went straight to voicemail. Brooke left a message to wish her happy holidays and tell her about the recording sessions, including the dates and times they would be doing the work. She'd closed by assuring her that she was more than welcome to stop by if she wanted. Given Cathie's notable absence all year, Brooke hadn't expected to hear anything back, so it came as a surprise when she looked up from the couch in the back of the booth, and saw Jason's mother heading down the corridor towards them. Brooke reached over and took Elissa's hand, giving it a tight squeeze as Cathie peered in the window and gently tapped on the glass.

Hannah was queueing up the next pre-taped transition when she spun around in her chair to wave 'hello' and inadvertently hit rewind on the reel to reel player.

"Oh shit!" Hannah exclaimed as the song on the air wound down to the final chords.

"What is it?" Elissa asked.

"I screwed up Hank's intros."

She looked into the studio, where the band was finishing a take. Hank was seated at the console with his eyes closed, bobbing his head along to the recording as it played back in his headphones.

Brooke held her index finger up to the window, telling Cathie to wait one second while they got things sorted out. "Can't you just do the segue yourself?" she asked Hannah.

"I don't know what songs are coming up. What would I talk about?"

"Just speak gibberish!" Brooke suggested. "That's all Hank seems to do."

By now, the music had completely stopped and the air had gone dead.

Out in the corridor, Cathie Pepper looked up at the silent speaker, realizing something was wrong.

The band had gone silent as well. Hannah ran over to the window that separated the broadcast booth from the recording studio. She pounded on the glass, trying desperately to get Hank's attention, but he couldn't hear her with his headphones on.

Grady looked over, watching Hannah's pantomiming antics as a bewildered smile spread across his face.

"This is *not* good!" Hannah shouted. "What do I do?"

"Imitate Hank!" Brooke said.

"No, no!" Elissa added. "Pretend to be Santa!"

Grady tapped Woodrow on the shoulder. Now the two of them were watching the chaos playing out on the other side of the glass. Soon Alvy and Asa had also become aware of the craziness. The only one oblivious to what was happening was Hank.

Hannah's finger wavered over the controls as she leaned toward the microphone. "Ohhhhh shit. OK. Here we go, " she muttered. Then she hit the button and went out live over the air. "Ho! Ho! Ho, kids!" She bellowed in the deepest voice she could summon up. "It's me. *Santa!* I hope you enjoyed that selection of *rockin'* tunes."

Brooke and Elissa were rolling on the couch with laughter. Out in the corridor, Cathie Pepper wore an expression of bemused horror.

"Uh, boss," Asa said as he tapped Hank on the shoulder and waited for him to take off his headphones. He pointed towards Hannah. "I'm not sure what's going on in there, but I think your woman has gone rogue."

Hank threw his headphones on the console and raced into the next room.

"I've been telling my reindeer friends to pick out all of their top tunes," Hannah continued. "Because I know you all want to have a *rockin'* Christmas Eve, just, like me, *Santa!*"

Hank burst into the broadcast booth and slid behind the microphone to take over.

"*Ooooooookay,* well thank you *Santa.* I'm not sure how you got in here, but I think I can take it from here," Hank said as he assumed the helm.

When he was done introducing the next batch of songs, he flipped the switch back to the music, and slumped back against the desk while the girls doubled over in laughter.

"You think it's funny, but I could get into a lot of trouble if anyone from the school found out I was letting some stranger take over the airwaves. They could lose their broadcast license!"

"Not some stranger," Hannah corrected. "Your *girlfriend.*"

Brooke motioned for Cathie to come in.

"I hope I wasn't the cause of that," Cathie said as she entered.

"Hey," Hank said. "I didn't know you were coming by."

"I just got back into town last night. Brooke left me a message to tell me what was happening, and when I heard the name of the band, I just knew I had to come down and see them for myself."

"Do you *know* the band?" Hank asked.

"Well, no. Not exactly," Cathie said as she raised a familiar looking bag from the floor and set it on the couch. Brooke recognized it immediately as Jason's old backpack. Cathie unzipped the top and reached inside. "But I remembered seeing something after I brought Jason's things home from the hospital. The minute I heard Brooke's message, I went into his room and grabbed this..." She withdrew a yellowed copy of *The Reporter*. It was folded open to the weekly live music listings from the week

Jason had died. At the bottom of the page was a notice circled with red ink. It read:

"This Saturday at The White Russian: Asa Flynn and the Fisher Cats LIVE!"

Hank studied the page and cracked a huge smile.

Jason Pepper had picked out their first band after all.

"That's perfect," Hank said to Cathie.

"I thought so too."

~

After the final sales were rung up, Karl went in the back and shut off the music. Loren, Kathy, Virginia, Dan, Jan, Mike, and Suzanne gathered around the main sales floor for a Christmas Eve huddle. They could hear Roxanne talking to her assistant as she made her way down the stairs.

"Tell Keith I'm handing out these bonus checks, then I'll start for home."

She emerged at the bottom of the stairs, where she was greeted by the staff's expectant faces.

"OK," Roxanne said as she realized everyone had just heard her conversation. "So, I guess I just gave away the surprise, but I have a little something for all of you to say thanks. This was the store's best holiday season *ever* and we owe much of it to your hard work and commitment. So, let me pass out these envelopes and we can all get out of here." Roxanne made her way around the circle, handing out envelopes. When she got to Loren, she paused and flashed an inscrutable smile.

"Thank you for everything," Roxanne said as she put her hand on Loren's shoulder. Then she pulled out an envelope, set it in Loren's hand, and moved on to the next person.

After Roxanne left, the remaining staff closed up the registers and locked up the shop. They exchanged hugs and 'Merry Christmases' in the back lot, then went their separate ways. Most headed home to be with their families. Loren set off towards the radio station to see how things were progressing.

~

Loren arrived at the studio just before the final push. They were down to the closing track and taking a moment to build up some steam for the last blast of work. Loren walked through the darkened corridors of WGRM, savoring the warmth and the relative quiet. The halls were decked out in radio-themed holiday décor. Green wreaths and gold records glittered in the dim light. When she stepped into the broadcast booth, she was met by the celebratory faces of her friends and the band.

Asa Flynn stood off to the side, sipping from a beer can, which he raised in quiet greeting when Loren looked over. Then he watched as Cathie Pepper walked over and gave her a long hug.

Asa turned to Brooke. "Can I ask you something?"

"Shoot."

"What's the story with Loren?"

"Why do you ask?"

"I've just sort of wondered what her situation is. She seems cool, and it doesn't seem like she's involved with anyone, but I get the sense that dating isn't on the table for her."

"First of all, yeah, she *is* pretty cool. But your sense is about right. She's working her way back from something that happened around this time last year."

"What?" Asa asked hesitantly.

Brooke took a deep breath, then quietly led him away to tell him about the accident.

Loren and Cathie joined Hank and Hannah at the recording console. Hank was playing them some samples and sharing his ideas for the final mixes.

"Honestly, Jason had a better mind for this part of the process," Hank told Cathie. "But I'm hoping to get it at least *halfway* right."

"It sounds great to me so far. I think he'd have loved it."

"I hope so," Hank said pensively. He looked up at the clock. "If we want to get this thing wrapped before Santa comes down the chimney, we'd better get cracking!"

Hannah stepped into the broadcast booth and called all the observers in to join her.

"Cathie, I hope you can stick around for the rest of the night," Hank said as he went into the studio with the band.

"I'll hang out for a little while longer," she said.

The band and Hank kicked back into high gear.

Cathie joined Elissa, Brooke, and Loren as they listened to the session and chit-chatted quietly. Hannah returned to her radio duties, rejoining the conversation after making doubly certain she wouldn't have any repeat mistakes with the taped introductions.

The night stretched on, and the vibe settled into a mellow, productive groove. As the energy from the music came to a head – signaling the sessions' approaching end – Cathie Pepper stepped to the back of the booth, grabbed her jacket, and gave the room an appreciative once over before she quietly slipped away into the night.

Hank removed his headphones as the final notes hung in the air. He looked around the room, studying the band's exhausted, satisfied faces. "And… I think that's a wrap!"

~

As the gang celebrated the conclusion of the recording sessions, the scope of what they'd accomplished grew increasingly clear, and with the weight of their work lifted, the spirit of the season settled over them. Eventually, as fatigue took over, everyone began to disperse, but not before plans were made to celebrate at the Fisher family's farm the next day.

"It's not fancy, but we throw a hell of a party," Alvy promised.

"Sounds good to me," Hank said as he shook hands with each of the guys before they left.

Asa lingered in the doorway as he was leaving, giving Loren a smile, "Will I see you there tomorrow?"

"I can't think of a reason you wouldn't," Loren said.

Brooke watched the exchange with a quiet, cautious half-smile.

After the band had left, the gang stuck around to help Hank shut down the station. Snow was falling as they stepped outside and looked around. They could hear the quiet rumble of The Falls behind the building. See the gentle shower of snow as the mist from the cascading water froze and billowed back over the campus in clouds of white powder. As Hank pulled the doors shut and locked them tight, he thought of Jason. Things that had been set into motion all those years before were reaching their inevitable conclusions. He looked around the group. They exchanged pensive smiles. Then they headed around the front of the building and started for home.

Hank and Hannah went back to their apartment at The Dean.

The girls went back to their place as well, where they visited in the glow of their Christmas tree for a short while before Elissa and Brooke snuck away to their room, leaving Loren alone with her thoughts. She stared into the warm glow of the Christmas lights and turned to watch the falling snow outside. This wasn't where she would ever have imagined herself one year ago. She wasn't necessarily happy, and this certainly wasn't the way she felt things should be, but as she sat in the warm darkness, Loren was comforted by the realization that, at least in this moment, she was at peace. And that was something.

* * *

"Merry Christmas!" Asa Flynn answered the door dressed in an outfit straight out of *A Christmas Carol:* a tattered, well-worn suit – complete with vest – embellished with a sprig of a holly and an old time Santa hat. He was holding a steaming mug of something.

"Wow, look at you," Hannah said as she and the rest of the gang streamed in.

"Very nice," Hank said. "Now I know what the cover will be when we run out of creative gas and record our first Christmas album."

"Don't even say that, Man," Asa said. "Don't even joke. Although… I can sing a mean Drummer Boy."

"Merry Christmas," Loren said, as she gave Asa a hug. "You look great."

"Thank you." He closed the door and followed her into the main room, where a band of old timers was playing music while friends and family danced and sang. Young kids were chasing one another around the room.

"Who's house is this, anyway?"

"This is Alvy's place. But I think he and his brothers all grew up here. It's the original farmhouse. Woodrow and Grady have places on the property too. You might have seen them."

"I did," Loren said, recalling the brightly lit houses they'd passed on their way up the long driveway. "Whose kids are these?"

"The guys'," he said with a shrug.

"Which guys?"

"The band. The brothers."

"They have kids?" Loren asked, surprised at this new bit of information.

"They each have multiple kids. And wives. Well, they each have *a* wife, and multiple kids."

"I would never have guessed that. Wow, their wives must be patient women to let their husbands record an album in the thick of the holiday chaos."

Asa laughed. "Why do you think the guys had no problem with Hank's off the wall scheduling?"

Loren surveyed the room and saw Woodrow dancing with a young girl, probably seven or eight years old, who was dressed in a pretty, homemade Christmas dress. When the music stopped, he picked the girl up in her arms, walked to the edge of the dancefloor, and kissed an attractive brunette in a matching dress. Grady crossed the room and put his arm around a striking blond dressed in what appeared to be a Mrs. Santa corset. Absurd as it sounded, she made it look *good.* They stopped under an elaborate bundle of mistletoe in the hallway and shared a passionate kiss.

"Is that Grady's wife?" Loren asked. "She's *gorgeous.*"

"Yep. Why do you think we all give him so much crap."

Loren shook her head. "Jealous men."

Asa smiled and took a sip of his drink.

"What do you have there?"

"This?" He asked, raising his steaming mug. "A Tom and Jerry. You want one?"

"Yeah. Why not?"

Asa led her through the crowd and into the kitchen, where a massive bowl of eggnog was set in the center of a butcher block island. Partygoers were dipping into the seemingly bottomless punchbowl of nog, and lingering in the kitchen, grazing on snacks and sweets. Asa cut a path through the thick of the crowd, and brought Loren over to a large red, green, and white punch bowl, filled with Tom and Jerry batter. He showed her how to ladle a portion into the matching mug, then he topped it off with hot water from a pot on the stove.

"Do you want rum or brandy?" he asked.

"What are you having?" Loren asked.

"I like a little bit of both."

"Then give me the same."

Asa finished preparing her drink, freshened his own, and they headed back into the main room to watch the celebration.

"This is delicious," Loren said as she took a sip.

"I'm glad you like it."

Elissa and Brooke crossed the room and joined them.

"Are these all Fisher family relatives?" Brooke asked.

"I think most of them are. Some are neighbors. I just know there are a ton of them. They asked me to bring over a *hell* of a lot of Tom and Jerry supplies."

"It's worth it," Loren said.

"What's worth it?" Hank asked, as he and Hannah came around the corner. "I hope you're talking about the album."

"The album is *definitely* worth it," Asa said.

The discussion shifted to what came next now that the recording was completed. There was still a lot to get done over the coming months.

Throughout the evening, Brooke caught Asa and Loren exchanging looks. He clearly liked her, and there was obviously some interest on Loren's part as well. Though Brooke doubted she was ready for anything to happen, it was encouraging to detect some inkling of interest on Loren's part.

The night wore on, the crowd thinned, children were slowly shuffled away to bed, and the Fisher brothers and their wives danced. They worked their ways around the room, making introductions and, of course, talking about the album. Finally, while Hank and Hannah were doing their best to sell the Fisher wives on everything they had planned for their husbands' music, Asa asked Loren if she wanted to dance. They slipped out into the middle of the room, circling the dancefloor to a quiet, almost mournful rendition of '*He Loves and She Loves*,' exchanging awkward smiles as the dance stretched on. It was a welcome change of mood when the band followed that song with '*Must be Santa*,' and the floor filled with the remaining Tom and Jerry-fueled revelers, singing and dancing like there was no tomorrow.

Loren couldn't remember the last time she'd felt so relaxed. She took Asa's hand and led him off the dance floor as the song ended.

"That was fun," she said.

"You're a good dancer."

"You are too."

"Look, I'm not sure what you know about my situation," Loren began as they slipped into the corridor. "I've had kind of a rough year-"

He nodded. "Brooke has told me."

"I'm not really looking for anything right now. But.. it's been really nice hanging out with you tonight."

"Same here," Asa said.

Loren stopped in the middle of the hall, still holding Asa's hand, as she glanced up at the mistletoe overhead. She looked back down and met his eyes. They hesitated, then exchanged a sweet, gentle kiss.

"Merry Christmas," she said

"Merry Christmas."

They returned to the group, and spent the rest of the evening talking quietly and enjoying their time with friends. When the night was over, and everyone was saying their farewells, Loren gave Asa an extra tight hug at the door, then she joined Hank and Hannah, and Elissa and Brooke for the snowy, moonlit walk back into town.

19.

Loren felt an overwhelming sense of accomplishment as she printed up the pages of her thesis and slipped them into an envelope to drop in Professor Taylor's mailbox. She knew there were a few sticking points still to be addressed, but no matter what happened from here on out, she had completed the bulk of her work. Anything she did from now until the end of the year would only serve to make it better.

Now she was ready for the next thing. Searching for inspiration for her follow-up project. That was the curious phenomenon, something her professors in The Writing Center had touched upon over the years. As a writer, it's one thing to complete a long-term project – that, in and of itself, is a terrific feeling – but the work is never done. There's a moment of celebration when your mind is clear and you're free to think of other things, to ponder life and goals and the road ahead, but inevitably the path leads on to the next idea. The subsequent step in your efforts to master the craft.

She was ready to tackle "the big one." What exactly that was, she didn't know. She had some ideas, and while a part of her wished to collaborate on something after spending so much time working on her own, she relished the idea of developing a story and building another structure all her own.

* * *

For someone so obsessed with grades and class rank through-out high school, Hannah had become a surprisingly indifferent student in college. That wasn't to say she was any less of a perfectionist now, only that she'd come to see academic acco-lades and GPAs as someone else's yardsticks for success. Her focus had shifted to her personal life. And though she initially fought it, she'd come to realize Hank's goals were also her own, not simply because she wanted him to succeed, but because she was every bit as invested in them as he was. She couldn't wait to get the label up and running, and she was confident in the band they'd picked for their first release. The album was turning out great, and she was determined to give it the best launch possible; the runup to its release was a dizzying experience, but she was relishing every step of the process.

She would still graduate on time, walking with her friends at the ceremonies in the spring, and though she feared she might have let her father down with her change of major, she sensed something was up with him as well. Calls and communications had fluctuated over the years, but in the last six months, Peter Merritt had clearly entered a period of decline. The part of her that once tried to distract from his problems with academic success held out hope that the lack of communication might mean he'd met someone, but in her heart, she suspected his battle with the bottle had once again taken hold. At some point, though she suspected he knew it already, she would have to confront Hank about similar issues, but that would open the door on a whole new side of their relationship, and *that* was a can of worms she was not yet ready to tackle. First the album, then the hard stuff. It sounded like the enabler's code, but she couldn't see any other way.

***

Loren saw Braden one final time.

She'd gone to the library with vague intentions, to finish some class reading and brainstorm new ideas. But in her heart of hearts, she knew she was there in the hopes that Braden might flare. A twinge in her stomach had pushed her to go.

And then, as she walked through the aisles of books, casually scanning the spines, she turned and saw that familiar smile.

"Hi, Braden."

"Hi."

"I was hoping to see you."

"Me too."

"Have you been here for long?" she asked.

"It's all relative, right? It feels like an eternity, and no time at all."

"We're almost to graduation."

Braden nodded.

"I finished my thesis," she said.

"Congratulations. That's a big deal."

"I wish you could read it."

His eyes glimmered. "Maybe I can one day."

"I'm figuring out what I want to write next."

"What about *Dead Men Don't?*"

"Our baby?" she asked with a little smile, using the nickname she'd always resisted.

"*Oh,* is it OK to call it that now?"

"I think, maybe it hit a nerve back then," Loren murmured. "You knew things I didn't."

"So what do you think? Do you want to finish our book?"

"I would love to, but I can't remember what we'd worked out. I'm not sure I could write it without you."

"What if you didn't have to?"

"I don't know what you mean, Braden."

"Look around the study hall, check the footplate beneath my desk."

She watched Braden's eyes blink in that curious, lagging manner she'd observed the last time.

"I left something you might find interesting," he continued. "And maybe you can do something with my novel. It's there too."

"*That's* where it is," Loren exclaimed. "I've been looking for your things ever since…"

"I put everything there before we left. You think I'd leave my writing in that fire trap of an apartment building? I found something else in there as well, something for Mark Price. He'll want to see it."

Loren remembered Ashton Study Hall's connection to Grimwood's infamous incident. "What is it?" she asked warily.

Braden shook his head slowly. "It's nothing sinister. I think it might give him some closure."

"Can you show me where to look?"

"You'll find it," he said as he started to drift back. "Don't worry."

"Braden?"

His eyes drifted up.

"I still love you."

"I'll *always* love you," he said before he vanished. "Goodbye, Loren."

Goodbye.

~

"It's nothing sinister."

Braden's words reverberated in Loren's head as she walked past the empty workspaces; they reminded her of one of their first conversations freshman year. When she reached Braden's preferred spot, she got down on her hands and knees and crawled under the desk. Their words once again echoed in her head as she searched.

"I don't want to write about sinister things."

"You don't want to tell dark stories, or you don't want to write about the bad things that can happen in life?" she'd asked.

"I guess both. People are here, and then they're gone. We can vanish in the blink of an eye and never see it coming. Why create stories that emphasizes how weak the threads holding all of this together really are?"

"Maybe to remind people that time is precious. Other than your life, what more do you have to lose? Dark stories can be cathartic."

"So, is that the kind of thing you want to say?" Braden had asked her.

"To be honest, I'm not sure what it is that I want to say I guess that's why I'm here…"

She wasn't sure what she was looking for.

He'd specifically said to look in this room. *This* was his preferred workspace. The floor was practically spotless with how little the space was used. Tales of those horrifying, long-ago events certainly kept visitors from exploring the library's upper reaches.

Check the footplate beneath my desk…

Loren shifted on the uneven, wide-planks. Her knee fell awkwardly on the edge of one of the floorboards. She winced, moving her leg suddenly and bumping the wood-paneled wall:

It reverberated with a hollow thunk. Loren turned, studying the intricate paneling with fresh eyes. She tapped on the wall with her fingertips, then with the palm of her hand, listening for the spots where the sound shifted, where the tapping was dampened. Then she felt along the bottom of the trim with her fingers until she found the detail she was looking for, a slight gap at the bottom of the tall baseboard, wide enough for a fingertip. She slipped her index finger into the space, lifted the board gently, and pulled it away from the wall. Once the baseboard was removed, the section of paneling above it shifted away from the wall slightly. Loren took ahold of it with both hands and pulled it away as well, setting it to the side as she peered into the hiding space tucked inside the wall.

Unlike the study room itself, this concealed space was thick with dust. The interior walls were covered with unfinished, dry wood, hammered into place with rectangular nails to form a secret cabinet, perhaps two feet wide, with the same height and depth. It wasn't a massive space, but it was big enough to hold three items stacked neatly in the center of the space, clearly Braden's methodical handiwork.

At the bottom of the pile was a thin leather binder, light tan and cracked with age and heat. Above that was a drawstring fabric bag. And on top of that was Braden's familiar old backpack. Loren studied the items, then she carefully slid them out of the cubby, climbed out from under the desk, and spread everything out on the tabletop beneath the light.

The binder looked like something a lawyer or a writer might carry. Loren wiped dust from the cover and turned it over. There, at the bottom right corner were two embossed words: Deborah Payne.

A shiver ran down Loren's spine as she recognized the name of Professor Price's late-fiancé, the key victim in Grimwood's infamous campus killings. Deborah Payne had been the object of the shooter's misguided and unrequited feelings, the young woman whose presence had inadvertently drawn him to the library all those decades ago with sinister if cloudy motivations.

Loren focused her thoughts, then she carefully opened the cover and removed a bundle of folded papers. A handwritten note across the top read: In the event of my death…

She spread out a collection of notes addressed to her parents and friends. The final pages were addressed to Mark Price. Loren looked over a few lines, before she realized what she was reading. When she recognized its meaning, she stopped reading, carefully placed the pages back in their original order, and returned them to the binder.

The second item was the drawstring bag in which Loren had kept all of the notebooks and materials she and Braden prepared for *Dead Men Don't*. Years ago, at the height of one of their infamous arguments, she'd taken all of their work and thrown it into the trashcan inside this very room, and they'd never really spoken of it again. Apparently Braden had retrieved it.

Loren took a seat, gently tugged the drawstrings open, and removed the contents. She recognized most of the items inside. The notebooks, held together with crumbling rubber bands. The pages of character outlines and notes. But there was something else inside, something she'd never seen before. The plan for their collaboration had involved the two of them writing alternating chapters in the book, with each of them working from a different point of view. At the bottom of the bag, fastened together with a heavy document clip, was an inch thick bundle of paper, with a cover page that read: *Dead Men Don't – a mystery by Loren Austin and Braden McNutt.* Loren folded back the cover page to find the completed first chapter. She flipped ahead and found a page marker for Chapter Two. Then she turned to Chapter Three. Again, she found it had been fully written. A marker for Chapter Four followed, along with the completed draft of Chapter Five And so on and so on. At some point over the intervening years, Braden had quietly resumed work on their great collaboration. He'd written all of his chapters, and carefully compiled everything they'd prepared together, so that one day, Loren could return to the project and write her half.

She leaned back in her chair, bowled over by the gesture. She'd been looking for her next big project, little did she know, Braden had it ready and waiting for her.

Finally, Loren unzipped Braden's backpack, where she found the bulk of the things she'd been looking for much of the last year, including his laptop computer, his notebooks, and a neatly-bound manuscript for Braden's completed novel.

After going through everything in the bag, Loren plugged in the laptop and started it up. On the desktop she found two folders. One was for his book, with the final document file carefully labeled front and center. The other was for *Dead Men Don't.* It too contained a file with Braden's completed passages, along with the place holders for Loren's yet-to-be-written chapters. A separate document contained a typed outline of everything the two of them had mapped out together.

Before she left the building, Loren sealed up the compartment beneath the desk. She took everything she had found with her. The drawstring bag and backpack were now hers. As for Deborah Payne's binder, *that* she would return to its rightful owner.

20.

The school year rushed onward, sweeping Loren along with it. She felt like a swimmer, paddling against the tide as it pulled her from Grimwood and out to deeper waters.

She was busier than ever. Between classes, shifts at the store, and completing the final revisions on her thesis, Loren was researching places to submit Braden's manuscript for publication. Most importantly, she was well on her way to completing her half of *Dead Men Don't*. It was the type of breathless, frenetic state of productivity she had always attributed to Braden, yet now it was her life.

On the first sunny day of spring, as the cold and damp were burning off, and the flowers were just beginning to push their way up through the soil, Loren slipped Deborah Payne's leather binder under her arm and headed for Mark Price's office. When she got there, she could see the professor through the door's window, seated at his desk, his back to the corridor as he worked. Not wanting to insert herself into the story any more than she and Braden had when they'd asked him about the incident years earlier, Loren ducked down and slid the binder under the office door with an audible *whoosh*. She heard the squeak of his desk chair and jumped to her feet, slipping into a group of students as they passed by. She stopped at the end of the hallway, just out of sight, and looked back to see Mark Price standing in his office doorway, studying the open binder in his hands. He looked up, giving the corridor around him one last sweeping view, then he gently removed the folded pages inside, stepped back into his office, and closed the door behind him.

* * *

"So, you're headed to the city?" Peter Merritt mused as he looked over the lunch menu.

"No, Dad, we're staying here,' Hannah said.

"I thought you said you were going to New York?"

Hannah watched her father's eyes as they drifted from the menu to the cocktail list tucked between the salt and pepper and the hot sauce. He was neatly dressed, his hair slicked back, clean shaven, but the closer she looked at him, the more Hannah noticed things were just slightly off. A line of missed whiskers on his neck. A smudge of dirt on his collar. For a man who'd always been fastidious about his appearance, it was the little things that set off the alarm bells.

"I said, 'depending on how things went here after graduation' – assuming we get some momentum going with the album – we *might* look at the city as we consider our next steps. That's a ways off though."

"That's terrific honey," he said, as he glanced at his watch.

It's was 11:00 a.m. , the day before graduation. They'd gone to Lola's for an early lunch, just Hank, Hannah, and her father, ostensibly to catch up and discuss about graduation, but Hannah couldn't help but think her father had requested the place in part because he remembered the bartender's generous pours.

"Hank, what are you thinking you'll have?" Peter asked.

"I'm not sure," Hank said as he met Hannah's gaze. "But the French dip is sounding pretty good."

"I was looking at that too."

Hannah waited, wondering if the conversation would return to their post-graduation plans, but her father's interest had shifted. He seemed preoccupied and itchy. He wasn't seeing anyone. It sounded like business was "not so dynamite." And his eyes kept darting back to that drink list.

When the waitress finally came by and took their orders, Peter waited until the last possible moment, like he was wrestling with himself over when to cross the threshold. After a final glance at his watch, he looked up with an exaggerated grin.

"And bring me a Manhattan while you're at it. It's not every weekend a man's daughter graduates from college."

~

"Are you certain you want to go to New York?" Rick Austin asked as he helped Loren tape up the moving boxes.

"That's the plan," Loren said. "If I'm gonna take a run at it, that seems like the place to do it."

"And you're *sure* you don't want to come home, maybe start up a new brewery with me?" her father asked.

"Rick, first of all, you aren't *allowed* to start a new brewery, at least not for the next four years," Mary Beth Austin said to her ex-husband. "Second, don't go putting doubts in her mind."

"I know," he said. "I just hate to see her stay back east."

Loren taped the flaps shut on her current box and looked up. It was funny, roughly two months after they sold Puzzlebox Brewing, her parents had finally gone through with their divorce, yet now they seemed to be completely at ease around one another. They'd arrived together one day earlier, and though they were staying in separate rooms at the same hotel, Loren she had yet to see either of them separately. It was just like their professional relationship now, comfortable, at ease, and strictly business. It seemed as though removing the pressure of the business and their marriage had reminded them that deep down they still enjoyed one another's company.

Loren was packing up the bulk of her books and clothing so that Hank and Hannah could send them down to her once she was settled. As she sorted through her things, she would stop now and then to flip open a book and read an inscription. Most of the nicer editions, particularly the Alan Grimwood titles, had notes from Braden. Those were the books she placed in her bags to bring with her.

"What are your friends doing after graduation?" her mother asked.

"Hank and Hannah are staying in town, for now. Brooke is going to Seattle with Elissa. Elissa got a job out there."

"What's she doing?" Rick asked.

"Working for some hot shot architect out there who is sort of her idol. Brook is playing it by ear until she gets there."

Loren stopped and looked around the largely-packed-up room.

"Four years went by pretty fast, didn't they?" her mother mused.

"Parts of them did. I guess it hasn't hit me."

~

Graduation was a blur of last minute preparations, gathering before the ceremony, taking pictures with friends and family.

Cathie Pepper was there with her boyfriend. She gave each of them a hug and wished them well. At one point, she took Brooke aside and gave her a gift.

There were family photos, last minute gown repairs.

Then, they were all seated in the audience, listening to the speeches and glancing back now and then to study familiar faces in the crowd; doing their best to experience everything in the moment, while simultaneously tucking away memories to look back on years from now – happy experiences to turn to when things weren't so simple, and life wasn't quite so fun.

Loren walked the stage in a daze as she went up to collect her diploma. She felt detached from her legs, a step removed from her body. Hands sweaty, afraid of stumbling. Then, just as quickly, she was back in her seat, absorbing the sounds of the crowd.

Four years.

All those days and weeks and months and *years*.

Friendships, loves, fallings out, and new beginnings. They would all be behind her soon. The mood was exciting and celebratory and surprisingly… sad.

Her thoughts were still in a haze when she filed out at the end of the ceremony and her friends slowly gathered to exchange hugs and congratulate one another on making it through.

"Let's meet up at Brick's tonight," Hank said as the group went their separate ways for the afternoon. "One more dinner, for old time's sake."

* * *

Brick's was quieter than usual. Most of the graduates were eating with their families at Grimwood's more high end establishments. Though it took some explaining to their parents, everyone in the group managed to get there on time. Betty brought their drinks and stuck around to congratulate them and wish them well in an uncharacteristically warm way. The dinner order was, of course, a round of Brick Plates for the table. That was a given. Betty headed back to the kitchen, and an unusual quiet came over the group.

"Jesus," Brooke deadpanned. "Did someone die around here?"

"Yeah," Loren said, joining in the gallows humor. "But not recently, so let's not push our luck."

Hank lifted his glass. "And on that note, a toast to the ones who couldn't be here. To Jason and Brady."

"Here, here."

Brooke looked around the table. "I wonder where we'll all be a year from now."

"If the albums crashes and burns, I'll probably be right here," Hank said. "Having a Brick Plate and wondering what the hell I was thinking."

"Even if things go according to plan, you'll *still* probably be here having a Brick Plate," Hannah noted.

"God willing, Hannah. God willing."

Their meals arrived and the conversation continued. Owing to the events of the past four years, everyone seemed well aware of uncertain promises and the fate of the best laid plans, yet on the whole, optimism was winning out.

They ordered a second and third round of drinks as the night stretched on. Finally, as the pressure to meet back up with their families grew, they made their way out to the sidewalk to say their goodbyes for the night, relieved to know they still had a couple more days to tie up loose ends before they scattered to the winds.

"When do you think we'll all be here together again?" Hank asked.

"At Grimwood or at Brick's?" Loren asked.

"Both."

"Probably the first reunion, whenever that is," Hannah said.

"Ten years?" Elissa asked.

"I'd hope to see you all sooner than *that*," Brooke added.

"There's nothing that says we can't get together whenever we like," Hank said before he and Hannah and Brooke and Elissa headed out.

Loren lingered behind. She wandered up the hill toward campus, making her way up the main drive, just as she had countless times before, slowly walking the campus and taking in sights she might not see again for years to come, if ever, depending on how the winds blew. Every corner of the campus held a memory. The overlook at The Falls, the Student Union, The Lookout and The Writing Center. And of course, The Library.

She headed down the quarter mile to the residential side, walking a loop around the darkening quad, looking up at each of the glowing dorm towers, nodding her head at passing underclassmen as they moved their things out for the summer. She studied Alan Grimwood's statue – forever standing watching in the center of the quad. Her thoughts, as always, returned to that moment with Braden. She was grateful the two of them had eventually gotten together, before that window closed forever.

Loren passed Brownie's and headed on toward The Avenue, once more walking along the lonely, wooded path where she'd long ago caught a fleeting glimpse of that familiar figure, forever surfacing on the campus that bore his family's name. If ever there were a reason to pursue one's life's work, Alan Grimwood embodied it. Unpursued passions, regret, the loneliness of potential never fully reached, Loren was determined to make the most of the opportunities before her. Braden had done his best to set her up with some additional runway. Now it was go time, and she planned to make the most of it. Unlike Alan

Grimwood, who would continue to observe future generations as they came and went over the ensuing decades, Loren was taking her years at the university with her to the next phase in her life. There would be no looking back. It was time to move onward.

***

Brooke ran her fingers over the small, green *Ninja Turtles* transistor radio Cathie Pepper had given her as a graduation gift. To an outsider, it would have seemed a very odd keepsake, but she remembered it from Jason's room. It had been one his most-prized possessions, a gift from his father.

"I thought you could put it on your drafting table," Cathie told her. "Something to remember him by."

As if she could ever forget.

Brooke held the radio in her hands, tracing the outline of the fading characters, then she wrapped it in a T-shirt and tucked it into the top of her duffel bag and headed outside. Elissa was packing things into the trunk of her car, focusing on the tasks at hand, a rock as always. The rest of the gang had come down to see them off that morning.

They were allowing themselves a week for the cross-country drive to Seattle. Not that there was any rush, the schedule allowed for detours if the opportunities presented themselves.

Brooke walked over to Loren. "If things work out, maybe I can check out your old stomping grounds in Arizona."

Loren took a deep breath before she spotted the faintest hint of a smile at the corner of Brooke's mouth and realized she was teasing her again.

Some things never changed.

And some things certainly did.

"Have a safe trip," Loren said as she gave her roommate a tight hug. It was hard to believe they hadn't been fast friends from the beginning.

Brooke had come a long way thanks to this circle of friends. Her goals for the future were unclear, but unlike the day she'd first arrived at Grimwood, she was optimistic about the future, open-minded, and ready to roll with the punches. There were no preconceived notions or rigid parameters for how things should play out. Opening herself up to possibility had likely saved her life. She would never have given Jason a shot, let alone Elissa, if she hadn't learned to set aside her bullshit rulebook all those years ago. Grimwood had been good for her. She knew that. And most importantly, she was happy now. That was everything.

"Let us know when you get there?" Hannah said as she hugged the two of them.

"Have a safe trip," Hank said.

"Good luck with everything, you guys," Elissa said as she got into the car. "And send us a copy of that record!"

Then they were off, pulling away from the curb as their three friends waved goodbye in the rearview mirror.

~

Loren sat in the back of Hank's car, watching the familiar sights go by as they drove to the train station. She glanced at Hank and Hannah in the front seat. Hannah was joking and smiling, absentmindedly reaching her hand over and playing with the curls of hair on the back of Hank's neck.

Maybe they *were* the couple that met in college and lived happily ever after. She hoped so.

Loren couldn't think of a time she'd ever seen Hannah so relaxed. She wasn't as hard on people anymore. She'd eased up on expectations and was more open to possibilities as they came along. She'd changed even more over the course of the last year, with many of those changes emerging as she and Hank fought to work things out between them.

Hank was also different now. He'd always been a naturally happy guy, but a slight wariness had crept into his personality. He was less prone to letting things fall into place on their own. Most importantly, he was focused. He and Hannah both were. *That* was what made Loren think they could very well make it for the long haul. With a common goal in their sights, they were increasingly like two peas in a pod. The same could be said for Brooke and Elissa.

That left Loren as the only member of the group who was heading into the next phase of her life alone, just like when she'd first arrived in Grimwood for her freshman year.

When they reached the station, Hank pulled Loren's bags from the trunk and walked them around to the sidewalk.

"We'll send your stuff down to the city as soon as you're ready," Hannah said.

"Don't be a stranger," Hank added.

"I won't be," Loren promised. "And maybe I'll see you guys down there."

Hank took a deep breath. "Fingers crossed."

Hannah nodded toward the entrance. "Do you want us to go in with you?"

"Nah, I'm fine."

And that was it.

Another round of goodbyes and she headed inside.

Loren could hear Hank's aging car rumbling away as she approached the ticket window. She bought a one way fare and walked across the quiet station to a long row of wooden benches, where she flashed back to a memory of Braden seated in that very spot, waiting for his train; the same train she was taking now. It was funny how life bookended itself again and again. She'd arrived alone, come through the doors just across the way, and started a new life in Grimwood, where she didn't know a soul. She'd made mistakes, reversed herself, and struggled to find her passion. Now, after years of life's up and downs and a lot of hard work, she'd said her farewells and was once more heading out on her own.

Loren raised a hand to her chest, running her fingers over the silver locket beneath her shirt.

Braden was gone.

She hoped he was at peace.

As for Loren, she was more determined, willful, and confident than at any other time in her life. Braden had played a big part in that, but it was the last year, during which she'd truly *fought* to find her own way, that had made all the difference.

"The eleven o'clock to Grand Central is boarding now." The announcement called out over the loudspeaker. *"All passengers, please board at track fifteen."*

Loren got to her feet, took one more look around, and headed out the door to the platform. She climbed aboard the train and took a seat where she could watch the familiar sights of Grimwood sliding past the window. When she no longer recognized anything coming into view, she took a pen and notebook from her bag, and began to work on something new.

About the Author

Mike Attebery is the author of ten novels, including *The Grimwood Trilogy*, *Chokecherry Canyon*, *Firepower*, *Seattle On Ice*, *Bloody Pulp*, and *Rosé in Saint Tropez*. He lives with his family on an island off the coast of Washington State.

You can find Mike online at:
www.facebook.com/AtteberyBooks/

on Instagram at
https://www.instagram.com/mikeatteberyauthor/

and on his website http://www.mikeattebery.com